Gables of Legacy

VOLUME TWO

A GUIDING STAR

a novel

ANITA STANSFIELD

Covenant Communications, Inc.

Cover image map © Photodisc, Inc./Getty Images

Cover design copyrighted 2002 by Covenant Communications, Inc.

Published by Covenant Communications, Inc.
American Fork, Utah

Printed in the United States of America
First Printing: October 2002

09 08 07 06 05 04 03 02   10 9 8 7 6 5 4 3 2 1

ISBN 1-59156-111-6

Prologue

When Tamra Banks joined the Church, her mother was angry. When she made the decision to go on a mission, her mother told her to never come back. She left everything behind to serve in the Philippines, but given the kind of family she'd come from, she tried to convince herself that it wasn't such a great loss. She'd been promised great blessings in her life if she would serve the Lord, but she never would have dreamed that her encounter with a couple serving in the same mission would eventually lead her to the life she was meant to live.

Michael and Emily Hamilton told her she would always have a place with them at their home in Australia. After two years of living with her aunt and immersing herself in genealogy, Tamra felt drawn to the Hamiltons' home, and the job they offered, by a force so strong that she couldn't deny the divine guidance of her decision to leave everything behind and accept their invitation. She quickly became fascinated by the Hamiltons' ancestors, who had lived and worked and died in the same home that was now dominated by their brooding and bitter son, Jess.

Tamra soon learned that more than two years earlier, Jess had been driving a car that had been hit head-on by a truck. The accident had killed his brother and sister-in-law, and his closest friend. After many months Jess's body had finally recovered, but it quickly became evident that his spirit was barely clinging to life. Tamra's attraction to Jess was as intense as her growing belief that she had been guided to *this* place to somehow help *this* man—if only he would let her. Acting on a prompting from the Spirit, Tamra was able to prevent Jess from succeeding with a suicide attempt. But coming to understand the source of such desperation proved far more difficult.

Jess's love for Tamra quickly became evident, and she fervently came to believe they were meant to be together; but the humility and openness Jess had exhibited following his brush with death soon dissipated into clouds of depression.

Tamra loved her work at the boys' home that had been owned by Jess's family for generations. She quickly learned to love Jess's family—those living as well as many of his ancestors whose lives she had the opportunity to explore through their journals and keepsakes. It was easy for her to imagine living out her life with him and his parents in the huge family home where generations of Jess's family had lived. But she wondered if it would ever be.

As the months passed, the distance between Tamra and Jess grew. Tamara prayerfully took advice from his great-great-grandmother's journal and gave him an ultimatum. Jess left home the next day, filling Tamra and his family with concern and dread. In spite of her deepest hope that Jess would eventually come to terms with his pain and be able to commit his life to her, Tamra decided to put some time and distance between them—to step back and see the full perspective of her life. Feeling the need to return to the States in hopes of making peace with her mother, she boarded a plane headed for L.A., wondering if she had turned her back on Jess forever.

Alone in a small motel room for days on end, and filled with despair, Jess finally forced himself to wade through his fears and get down on his knees. Following days of fasting and prayer, he finally found perfect peace in the healing gift of the Atonement. He returned home a changed man, only to find Tamra gone. With a prayer in his heart he set out to find her and discovered she had taken a flight to the States. He managed to get a seat on the first available flight out and coincidentally found Tamra on the same plane.

With the evidence of Jess's change of heart, Tamra found incomparable joy in his dramatic marriage proposal aboard the plane. They talked and shared their plans for the future until the cabin lights were dimmed for the night, and they drifted off to sleep, hand in hand.

Chapter One

Tamra felt the low hum of jet engines before she came fully awake and realized it was early morning. She'd drifted in and out of sleep with odd dreams, always waking to find Jess's hand still in hers. With morning light trickling into the plane cabin, she watched him while he slept, in awe of the miracles that had brought them to this point. With his dark, wavy hair rumpled, and his face showing a shadow of dark stubble, he'd never looked more adorable. She thought of all the fasting and prayers on Jess's behalf by so many who loved him, as well as the many temples where his name had been put on prayer rolls. Tamra's testimony of the power of prayer deepened as she tried to comprehend the feelings and experiences that had led her to this point in her life. She contemplated the many stories she had read in Jess's ancestors' journals and all she had learned from them. She knew beyond any doubt that they had been brought together with some help from the other side of the veil—most especially Jess's great-great-grandmother, Alexandra Byrnehouse-Davies. Tamra felt a deep kinship with this woman, and she knew in her heart that Alexa would be pleased with the progress they had made.

She couldn't hold back a soft little laugh as her joy just seemed to overflow.

"What's funny?" Jess asked without opening his eyes.

"I thought you were asleep."

"I thought *you* were asleep," he said and opened his eyes to look at her. They were neither blue nor green, and there was a new sparkle in them. The darkness that Tamra had seen there through most of their relationship was gone. He smiled and kissed her quickly. "Good morning, the future Mrs. Hamilton."

Tamra grinned. "Good morning."

Jess reached up a hand to touch Tamra's lightly freckled skin, wondering how he could have been such a complete fool by almost letting her slip away. Reminding himself that the past was behind them, he uttered a silent prayer of gratitude that they were together at last, and the future before them was bright.

He watched her reach into her bag and pull out a hairbrush, which she maneuvered through her long, wavy red hair. It was the most beautiful hair he had seen in his life, and he couldn't resist running his hand through it, following the trail of the brush. She smiled toward him before she efficiently pulled all of her hair together and twisted it into a clip that she fastened at the back of her head in her usual way. She pulled out the familiar tube of wine-colored lipstick and smoothed it on in a few seconds without any mirror or fuss. As far as he knew, it was the only makeup she ever wore, and he loved the way she seemed to have too much life to live to bother with such things.

After they landed in L.A., Tamra was relieved when Jess was able to get a seat on the same flight she already had a reservation for. En route to Minneapolis, Tamra's hometown, it suddenly struck her that Jess Hamilton was going with her to see her mother. Besides the fact that she had no idea how her mother was going to respond to seeing her again, Tamra knew her mother's lifestyle and circumstances were anything but desirable—or admirable. She thought of Jess's family and the love she'd felt in his home. The contrast to where she was taking him now made her nauseated. She'd told him the situation, and he'd met her Aunt Rhea, who lived in Sydney. But how could she explain that her mother had gotten the worst of whatever Rhea had gotten the best of? Stewing about it only made Tamra more nervous and upset. She had to face it head-on, and the hours before their arrival were dwindling quickly.

"Jess," she said, "I need to talk to you about something."

"Ooh, it sounds serious," he said, looking up from the magazine he was reading, then closing it and setting it aside. "Don't tell me. Don't tell me. You have a lifelong dream of owning a pet chimpanzee, and you're afraid my parents won't tolerate it in the house. Well, not to worry, my dear. We'll just keep it in our room, and they'll never know. You can have a whole jungle in there, for all I care."

Tamra laughed and lightly slugged him in the shoulder. "Where did you learn to be so silly?"

"I have no idea," he said.

"Okay, now can I talk to you?"

"I'm listening."

"Jess, you realize that my purpose for this trip is to see my mother."

"Yes."

"And . . . when I got on the plane, I really hadn't planned on having you with me."

He looked more than a little alarmed. "I'm sorry. I didn't even think about . . . I mean . . . if you don't want me to—"

"No, Jess. It's okay. I'm glad you're with me. If we're going to be married, you should meet my family—what there is of it. But . . . I'm not proud of what I came from, and taking you to see it is . . . well, it's embarrassing."

"Whoa. Whoa. Wait a minute. *What's* embarrassing?"

"Whatever situation or mood we may find my mother in, I can assure you it will not be favorable. She can be more offensive than an R-rated movie. But she's my mother, and I know in my heart that I have to do this. I have to do my best to make peace with her. And whether or not she will accept my gesture is up to her."

"What you're doing is admirable, Tamra. I would love to meet your mother, but if you want me to wait at the hotel, or—"

"No, I don't. I . . . Well, quite honestly, I want her to meet you, because you are amazing in every sense, and . . ." She hesitated when her thoughts stirred uncomfortable memories.

"What?" he asked gently, touching her chin.

"About the time I joined the Church, my mother brought home a new man. It was their first date. He spent the night. I was disgusted, and I was immature. I called her a tramp. She told me if that was the case, then I had been raised by a tramp, and I was a fool to believe that my life could ever be any different than what she had lived. She said that changing my religion would never change who or what I am, and one day I would be passing myself from one loser to another the way she was. She considers the ideal catch to be rich and handsome. She never got a rich one. She rarely got one that even had a job. She got handsome a few times, but they were the ones who treated us the worst."

Tamra sighed and wrung her hands. "My mother is judgmental and rude, Jess. It will only take her about half a second to see that you're adorable." She smiled at Jess then looked back at her hands. "And I don't care if she finds out that you're rich, even though she'll probably start trying to figure out how she can get a loan that she'll never pay back. And anything else she might learn about you will be irrelevant—at least to her. So, what I'm trying to say is that . . . it's probably immature and silly, but . . . I want her to know that she was wrong. I wouldn't care if you were dirt poor and ugly as sin. I would be proud to take you to meet my mother, if only to let her know that I have won the love of a good man who will love and respect me for the long haul."

"You'd better believe it," he said firmly.

"And maybe I just want to be able to stand up to my mother appropriately, not with the anger and immaturity I displayed toward her before I left. I want her to know that I'm not the loser she expected me to be."

"Sounds reasonable," he said.

She smiled and added, "So, I kind of got off on a tangent there, but . . . I guess what I'm saying is . . . well, I just don't want you to think less of me because my mother is so—"

"Now listen, Tam," he interrupted. "I've told you before, my love, one of the many things that makes you so amazing is the way you have risen above the worst kind of upbringing to become such an incredible woman. I sank below the best kind of upbringing to become a loser."

"And I've told *you* before, my love, you are not a loser."

"Not anymore," he said earnestly. Looking into her eyes, he added, "Because I'm not going to let myself be a loser anymore, Tamra. You deserve better than that." He leaned closer and smiled. "Do you want to know how I know I'm not a loser?"

She smiled in return. "I would love to know."

"Because God loves me. And the only real losers in this world are the ones who have no comprehension of that love. And that's why I *was* a loser, and why I'm not going to be one anymore. And you, my dear, were *never* a loser. You grew up looking at all the losers around you, knowing you didn't belong. You are the cream of the crop, the pick of the litter. You are like a beautiful swan swimming zealously upstream, while all the ugly little ducklings just float downstream into the muck."

Tamra chuckled. "I think that was probably the greatest compliment I've ever been given—not necessarily the most poetic, but very sweet."

"Hey," he shrugged, "I have my talents. Poetry isn't one of them."

"I'll tell you what one of your talents is."

"What's that?"

"You have this incredible ability to make me feel more beautiful and more valuable than I have ever felt in my life—now that the real you has finally come through."

Jess touched her face and gazed at her with adoring eyes, as if to affirm what she had just said. "That's not hard," he said. "And you know what? It doesn't matter what your mother says, or does, or even implies. I spent a lot of time in my youth in questionable company, so I know people like that. She can curse at me, blow smoke in my face, get drunk or stoned and make a complete fool of herself, and it will not shock me. And it will not make me feel any differently about you."

Tamra sighed deeply and tried to believe him. "Then I guess everything's going to be okay. It might be an adventure, but it will be okay."

"Yes, it will," he said, "even if I'm not ugly." She laughed and he added, "I could maybe, I don't know, shave my head or something, and glue some of those phony warts on my face and get some really dorky clothes and—"

"That's okay," Tamra chuckled and kissed his nose. "I like you just the way you are."

"Well, the feeling is mutual," he said.

They arrived in Minneapolis late and Tamra felt exhausted. By the time they had rented a car and found a decent motel, she could hardly keep her eyes open. She went with Jess into the motel office while he checked in, asking for two nonsmoking rooms as close together as possible. When he pulled his credit card out of his wallet to pay the bill, Tamra said, "You don't have to pay for all of this, you know. I actually have money for this trip, and if you hadn't come along I would have—"

"Managed just fine, I know. But you're practically my wife, Tamra Sue, so now seems just as good a time as any to let me start taking care of you. If I didn't have the money, we'd have to quibble over the bill. But I've got it, so . . . save your money and buy something useful with it, like . . . a chimpanzee, or something."

"You must be even more tired than I am," she said. "You're becoming giddy."

Jess helped carry Tamra's luggage into her room, then he kissed her good night and she locked the door behind him. She hurried to find her pajamas and toothbrush, then she said her prayers and crawled into bed, grateful to know that her *fiancé* was sleeping two doors down.

Tamra awoke after ten, feeling well rested and anxious to be with Jess. While she took a quick shower and got dressed, she remembered her reason for being in Minneapolis, and knots tightened in her stomach. She thought of the landmarks she'd seen coming into the city last night. Perhaps she'd been too tired to absorb the reality then, or maybe she'd been in some level of denial. But now it struck her fully that she had returned to the city where she'd grown up, and there was hardly a good memory to be found.

Brushing through her wet hair, the memories took hold more fully, and she began to doubt the wisdom of even coming here. She'd made the decision on an impulse, and at the time she had believed it was a prompting, but now she truly wondered. Still, she'd come this far. And deep down inside she really *wanted* to take this step with her mother, if only to be able to press forward in her life, knowing that she'd tried. All she had to do was walk into the bar her mother owned, say hello, ask how she was doing, and walk back out. She nearly had herself talked into it when a knock at the door startled her, reminding her that she had not come to this city alone, and there was no simple way to get through this day.

Not wanting to pull Jess into her internal drama, she took a deep breath and called in a cheerful voice, "Who is it?"

"The maid," Jess answered.

Tamra called back, "I don't trust a motel that hires Australian men to clean their rooms."

Jess laughed and she opened the door. He stepped in and closed the door quickly. "It is *freezing* out there."

"Yes, well . . . it *is* November."

"November?" he asked, genuinely surprised. "It's November?"

"It is."

"I must have lost more days lying around that stinking motel than I'd thought."

"At least lying around that motel room finally brought good results," she said, recalling the details he'd shared of his spiritual experiences there.

He smiled at her. "And now I'm here with you, and it's November."

"Good morning, Jess," she said.

He pulled her into his arms and gave her a kiss that almost dispelled the uneasiness hovering inside of her. Almost.

"Good morning," he replied in a dreamy voice and kissed her again. He stepped back and cleared his throat. "Your hair's wet, Tamra Sue. You'd better get it dry or it will freeze and break off out there. I don't think it was ever this cold in Utah."

"Probably not," Tamra said. "But then, deep down, your blood is conditioned for Australia."

"Yours probably is too," he said, "considering you haven't been here since before your mission. How long has that been? Five years?"

"About that," she said.

"And I don't want you to get sick, so . . ." He stopped and narrowed his eyes, looking into hers deeply. She glanced quickly away, not wanting him to see the truth of what she was feeling. "What's wrong?" he demanded.

Tamra turned her back to him. She'd become accustomed to him being so absorbed in his own pain and fears that she wasn't certain how to handle this newfound perception. While she was searching for an answer that would prevent her from having to make explanations she didn't even want to think about, he turned her around to face him, and put his hands firmly on her shoulders. "What's wrong?" he asked again, bending only slightly to meet her eye to eye. At six feet tall, Jess had only a slight advantage over Tamara's five-foot-ten frame.

"Tamra?" he pressed, but her head was so full of confusion and uncomfortable memories that she couldn't find her voice at all. "Are you concerned about seeing your mother?" he guessed and she nodded, totally unprepared for the flood of emotion that erupted. She found her face against Jess's shoulder while he rubbed the back of her head and tried to soothe her. Instinctively she clung to him, reminding herself that Jess was tangible evidence that she was putting the past behind her.

When she finally calmed down, he looked into her eyes and said gently, "Now, do you want to tell me what's going on?"

"No, but I guess I should."

"*You're* the one who told me I needed to talk about the things that were eating at me."

Tamra slumped onto the edge of the bed, her face in her hands. "I don't know what's wrong, really. I just . . . don't want to do this. I don't want to be here."

"Well then . . . let's go. Nobody said you had to do it."

Tamra sighed. "But I do. Deep down I know I have to try."

"Okay," he said, "then let's just do it and get it over with."

Tamra said nothing, and didn't move. Jess sat on the edge of the bed beside her. "Would you be more comfortable if I stayed here and just let you go and—"

"No," she insisted. "I mean . . . the thing is, I want my mother to meet you. I just don't want *you* to meet *her.*"

Jess's sigh brought home to her the ridiculousness of the statement even before he said, "It's up to you, Tamra. I've told you how I feel about this. Nothing I see or hear today is going to change the way I feel about you. But if you want me to stay here and wait for you, I will."

Tamra quickly weighed her choice and had to admit, "I really don't want to do this alone."

"Well, then," he said, "let's just go do it." When she didn't make any attempt to stand up, he added, "You know what I think?"

"What?"

"I think you're thinking too hard about it. Why don't you just go and do what you came here to do, and you can analyze it later. I can understand why this is difficult, but maybe you're making it harder than it has to be."

"Maybe I am," she admitted and sighed again. "Okay, I just need to do it. I'll never forgive myself if I leave here without at least trying."

"That's the spirit. Now, let's get going. I'm starving. That dinner on the plane stopped being useful a long time ago, so hurry and dry your hair. And then we're going shopping before we do anything else."

"We are?" she asked, grateful for a distraction.

"Yes, I need a coat. I packed light, and I packed in Australia— where it was *warm*. Hurry up."

Tamra dried her hair while Jess flipped through television channels. When she was ready she put on her jacket and said, "Okay, let's go. Hurry up. I'm starving."

He grinned at her and flipped off the TV. "You okay?" he asked gently.

"I will be, I think," she said and reached out to take his hand.

Walking to the car, she shivered and exclaimed, "Ooh, it *is* cold."

He glanced at the jacket she was wearing and said, "Looks like you need a coat, too."

After sharing a big breakfast, Tamra told him where to find a Target. They ran from the car to avoid being in the cold air any longer than necessary. As Jess grabbed a cart and pushed it toward the clothing department, he said, "So, what's your plan? After we get you a coat, that is."

Tamra pushed down the uneasiness that welled up inside her all over again. She reminded herself of Jess's advice; she would just do it and analyze it later. Still, she had to admit, "Well, I'd like to put off seeing my mother as long as possible, if you want to know the truth. I'm really dreading it."

"Then it would be better to get it over with."

"Which is exactly what I was thinking."

"So, when?" he asked.

"The middle of the afternoon would be best, I think," she said. "She and my brother will both be at the bar, and it will be practically empty that time of day."

Jess glanced at his watch and said, "We have plenty of time for shopping."

"So we do," she said. "But just so you know, *I'm* paying for my own coat, and I might pay for yours too." Before he could protest she added, "If I'm practically your wife, then it really doesn't make any difference, right? It's not your money or my money; it's *our* money. And I want to spend some of *our* money at Target."

"Yes, ma'am," he said, trying to imitate an American cowboy, which made her laugh.

They each picked out coats that were adequately warm without being too bulky for travel. Tamra found a special display of hats and gloves and picked out a black fleece set with little white snowflakes embroidered on them. She tossed them into the cart just before Jess picked up a pair of gloves for himself and said, "And you can buy these for me, too."

She smiled as he picked up a fleece hat in a bright-pink, loud print. The three floppy points made it look very much like a jester's hat. He tried it on Tamra, grinned, and said, "And you can buy that, too."

He tossed it into the cart and she said, "Careful, Hamilton. I'm not your wife yet. What makes you think I want that hat?"

"I'm getting it for you," he said, "with *our* money." He added in a whisper, "And I'm well aware that you're not my wife yet. If you were, we would only have *one* motel room."

Their eyes met with a meaningful glance and Tamra was filled with butterflies at the very idea of being Jess Hamilton's wife. She distracted herself by finding a jester hat that fit him, then added it to their purchases.

"And we need scarves," she said, recalling the bitter winters of her youth.

"Scarves?"

"Absolutely. You can't breathe in much of that cold air."

"Scarves," Jess said decidedly as they came upon some. He picked out two that went well with the coats.

"Okay," he said, looking around, "but what if it snows?"

"What makes you think it's going to snow?"

"Did you see the weather report?" he asked. "No, you were drying your hair. What if it snows?"

"What if it does?" she asked.

He looked down at the loafers they were each wearing on their feet before he marched them to the shoe department and picked out some matching lace-up boots—on sale.

"Can you afford all of this?" he asked.

"I sure can. I had a great job back in Australia at that boys' home, and I didn't have anything to spend my money on because I had great room and board benefits, as well."

In a sober tone he asked, "Why exactly did you leave that great job?"

"Shirley came back," she said in reference to the woman on maternity leave whom she had temporarily replaced at the boys' home.

"I'm sure there was something you could have done."

"Yes, I'm sure there was. Murphy told me I could help keep the strappers in line."

Jess chuckled, imagining Tamra working with the stable master and hired hands. "I'm sure you could, but you probably wouldn't appreciate their language."

"If I was keeping them in line, they wouldn't be using that kind of language." He smiled and she added, "What you're really trying to ask is, why did I leave?"

"That's right," he said.

"Well, I guess I just had to get some space and be certain that if I ended up staying there, I was doing it for the right reasons. I had no way of knowing if you and I would end up together, and . . . I guess I just had to find myself before I made any big decisions."

Jess stopped her in the middle of the office supplies aisle and took both her hands. "Did you find yourself, Tamra?"

"I did. I found myself in the temple, Jess. That's where I knew that I needed to try and make peace with my mother, and I knew that I would be all right—whether you came back into my life or not." She touched his face and added, "I would have been all right, but never truly complete. I truly found myself when I found you sitting next to me on that plane."

"Funny," he said, "that's where I truly found myself too."

She kissed him quickly and moved on through the store, fearing she might break down and cry otherwise. She just felt so perfectly happy—until thoughts of seeing her mother intruded on her bliss. Then she almost hated herself for wondering if such happiness was just too good to be true for a woman with her upbringing. Trying to push such thoughts away and enjoy the moment, she took hold of Jess's hand, hoping the contact would help her keep her perspective.

They each added some junk food and soda to the cart, and then to kill some time they perused the electronics section, and even the toys. Jess found a three-dollar Lego set with pieces to construct a little motorcycle. He tossed it into the cart and answered her questioning gaze by saying, "I've got to have something to play with."

Tamra paid for the purchases with her card that would take the money out of her checking account back in Australia. "Thank you," he whispered while she was signing the receipt. "Especially for the Legos."

"You're welcome," she said. Before going outside they cut the tags off their coats, scarves, and gloves and put them on.

"Much better," Jess said as they stepped outside.

They put their packages into the trunk. Jess closed it and took Tamra in his arms, kissing her long and hard. When his kiss ended, Tamra smiled at him and said, "You know why Eskimoes kiss by rubbing noses, don't you?" He looked confused and she added, "Otherwise, their lips would freeze together. You'd better get in the car before we end up frozen together and become a public spectacle."

He laughed and opened the car door for her. He drove for several minutes without asking for any directions, then Tamra noticed he had an address and some directions on a little piece of paper that he kept glancing at. He'd obviously been making some calls this morning from his room. When he pulled the car up in front of a jeweler, she asked, "What are we doing?"

"We're going to look at rings," he said. "If we're engaged, then your left hand ought to look the part, don't you think?"

Tamra couldn't help being pleased as he opened the door for her and led her into the little shop. Like most every girl, she'd dreamed of the day when she could wear a diamond that symbolized the love of a good man. He told the woman behind the counter that they just wanted to look for a few minutes and she left them to it. Perusing the dozens of different wedding sets in the glass cases, Jess pointed at a ridiculously overbearing one and asked, "How about that?"

"Oh, it's gaudy and vulgar," she said, glad to see that he'd obviously been teasing.

They looked for several minutes before he said, "Try that one on."

"Ooh, it looks expensive," she said.

"But it's not gaudy and vulgar," he said, and she laughed.

"No, but . . . I'm really not into jewelry, Jess. I don't know if—"

"This is not *jewelry*," he said. "This is the ring you will wear for the rest of your life to tell the world that you're married. I know it's pretty insignificant in the eternal scheme of things, but it's . . . well, it's part of our culture, I suppose. And you should have a beautiful one, because that's what our love is—it's beautiful."

He said to the woman waiting at a polite distance, "I'd like her to try that one."

"Oh, Jess, that one's too expensive," she said, wishing he hadn't been perceptive enough to notice how she'd been drawn to it for reasons she couldn't explain. On either side of the diamond solitaire, set in yellow gold, were two tiny rubies. She'd always liked rubies, even though they weren't her birthstone.

Jess slid the ring onto her finger and declared it a perfect fit. She hesitated to admit how thoroughly she liked it. But she feared he could see the truth in her eyes. It was far more showy than anything she'd ever owned in her life, but it made her feel beautiful somehow. And yes, loved. Still, she had to admit, glancing over the other rings on display, almost any one of them would have the same effect. A point she felt compelled to clarify. "It is beautiful, Jess, but—"

"You like it, don't you?"

"I do, but . . . I like a lot of them, and . . . it doesn't have to be expensive to—"

"We'll take it," Jess said to the woman.

"Jess," she protested quietly, "you can't just—"

"Yes, I can," he said. "And I just did."

"But, Jess, it's—"

"Listen to me, Tamra," he said taking her shoulders into his hands, "if we couldn't afford a ring like this, we wouldn't get it. But we can, and I really like it." He lifted her hand to admire the way it sparkled there. "It just seems . . . right. Now tell me honestly, do you like it or don't you?"

"I love it, but—"

"We'll take it," he repeated to the saleswoman who was hovering at a distance, as if she sensed their disagreement, even if she couldn't hear what they were saying.

Tamra sighed and told herself to be gracious. She looked again at the ring and couldn't deny the delighted little tremor inside her.

Back in the car, she admired her left hand again and said, "You didn't buy this ring to impress my mother, did you?"

"Will it impress your mother?" he asked, as if he didn't care.

"Very much," she said. "But that's not why I like it."

"And that's not why I bought it," he said.

"But you stopped to buy it *before* we went to meet her, and—"

"And if the ring you wanted had needed to be sized, we would not have been able to take it today. But I'm glad it fit, because I must admit that I want your mother to see tangible evidence that you're engaged, which means that buying a ring is more practical *before* our visit as opposed to *after*. But let me clarify something. I didn't buy that ring so people would be impressed."

Tamra thought of how Jess had a way of wanting to be different from the crowd, and a little bit flamboyant. But she knew from experience that it was not for the purpose of trying to impress anybody; it was simply part of who and what he was. She smiled to think of how they'd once attended a party together, extremely overdressed—and that was the way he'd wanted it, just because he thought it was more fun. She took his hand and asked, "Would this concept have anything in common with wearing formal clothes to a casual affair?"

He smiled. "Exactly. But this is more important. You see . . ." He hesitated, wishing he could explain it without sounding like an idiot. "Hey, did you ever see that movie in seminary about the—"

"I didn't go to seminary," she said. "I joined the Church when I was eighteen."

"Oh, yeah. Well, there's this little movie made by the Church called *Johnny Lingo* and—"

"Oh, I've seen that . . . at a group family home evening thing."

"Okay," he said eagerly. "Then you understand."

"Understand what?"

"That ring is not a skinny cow that gives sour milk; that is an eight-cow ring."

Jess sighed when she obviously didn't understand. "Tamra," he said, "your mother wanted you to believe that you were worth nothing of any value to any man—like the woman who would not be worth even a skinny cow that gave sour milk. That ring is to help *you* remember every time you look at it, that to me, you are worth everything I have, and everything I am. Whatever anybody else thinks of it is irrelevant to me, beyond it being the symbol that you are very much taken. That ring is for *you*—because I love you."

Tamra was surprised by, but not ashamed of, the tears that came to her eyes.

"What's wrong?" he asked.

"You're doing it again, you know."

"Doing what?" he asked. "Am I overbearing? Obnoxious? What?"

"No, Jess. You're making me feel valuable again; you just have a way of doing that—without even trying."

"It's like I said before." He reached over and took her hand. "It's not hard."

They drove for a few minutes in silence while she began to think of their destination and got knots in her stomach all over again. Searching for a distraction, she said, "So how are you doing, driving on the other side of the car?"

"Just fine, thank you. I've spent a lot of time in the States, you know."

"Yes, I know," she said. Most of his college education and his mission had been in Utah.

"However," he said, "do you know why the Siamese twins went to Australia?"

"No, why?" she asked, wondering about the relevance of such a question.

"So the other one could drive," he said, and she laughed so hard that she forgot all about her nervousness until he told her she needed to give him directions.

She told him where to turn, then said, "I really liked your joke."

"Yes, well . . . it's probably not politically correct, but in a family of Australian Americans, or American Australians, depending on which one of us you're talking to—that joke has gotten a lot of mileage."

"I dare say it has," she said.

"I love you, Tamra."

"I love you too, Jess."

"Then everything's going to be okay," he said.

She forced a smile and said, "I'll have to take your word for it."

The absolute delight of the morning dissipated into a dark dread as Jess followed her directions past familiar landmarks, toward the part of town where her mother lived and worked. Memories she had trifled with earlier that day rushed at her in torrents, and most of them were ugly. She did her best to stay focused on the moment, praying that she could get through the next hour without falling apart or screaming.

"That's it on the right, where that red car is parked. There's parking in the rear, but this time of day you can probably find a place . . ." She stopped when he pulled up almost directly in front of the door. "Yeah, right here," she said.

He turned off the engine and she had to say, "I really don't want to do this."

"It's going to be okay, Tamra. All you can do is your best. When you have absolutely no relationship with her at all, you're not jeopardizing much here. If she's obnoxious, then we say, 'It's been nice seeing you. So long.' And you'll know you tried."

"Okay," she said and took a deep breath. "Let's get it over with." He moved to get out of the car and she added abruptly, "No, wait. I need a minute." Trying to get herself geared up, she envisioned the scene inside the bar. "My mother is probably sitting on a bar stool, smoking a cigarette, doing a crossword puzzle in the back of some sleazy magazine. And my brother will be standing behind the bar, polishing glasses like they did in the old westerns." She laughed tensely. "I think he considers himself the proverbial bartender; it's his calling in life. They'll be casually gossiping about their customers, picking at everyone's faults and problems, as if it might make their own pathetic lives seem a little better."

"Sounds fun," he said with sarcasm. He put his arm up on the back of the seat and ran his fingers through her hair that was pulled into a ponytail. "But you know what?"

"What?"

"You made some very courageous choices that got you away from such a lifestyle." He kissed her quickly. "And I'm sure glad you did. Let's go in there and see how they're doing, then we can get on a plane and go home." She said nothing and he added, "How about a prayer?"

Tamra looked into his eyes, wondering if he had any idea how grateful she was to be loved by such a man. He had come so far in reawakening the spiritual depth that she had always believed was an innate part of him.

"That would be great," she said, and they discreetly bowed their heads. Jess held both her hands tightly while he prayed aloud that

Tamra would be strengthened to face this difficult situation. He expressed his appreciation for their being together, and for the love they shared. He expressed sincere gratitude for the blessings they enjoyed in their lives, and especially for the recent events that had assured both of them of the power of the Atonement. Jess prayed that he and Tamra would be guided to say the right things, and that her mother's heart would be softened and they would be able to heal the old wounds.

After the amen, Tamra looked up to see her tears mirrored in Jess's eyes. She wiped them away and blew her nose. "Okay," she said, "let's go."

Jess got out and opened the door for her. He helped her out of the car, then he took a lingering glance at her left hand before he kissed it. "Beautiful ring," he said. "Somebody must love you very much."

"Yes, somebody does, but I don't need a ring to know that."

"Then it was worth every cent," he said, and they went into the bar. Jess noticed the way Tamra opened and closed the door carefully, as if she didn't want to alert anyone to her presence. The aroma brought keen memories to his mind of lingering in crowds where liquor and cigarette smoke were prevalent.

Just as Tamra had predicted, the place was almost deadly quiet, except for the music playing in the background. A quick glance told him it wasn't a terribly classy establishment, but it wasn't the kind to attract the real lowlifes, either. Only a few steps beyond the door, Tamra hesitated and squeezed his hand tightly. Jess had to suppress a chuckle when he saw the exact scene that she had described. The *proverbial bartender* was slightly stocky, with a mustache and subtly wavy hair—exactly the color of Tamra's. The woman smoking at the bar looked very much like her sister, Rhea, except perhaps older in the face. They had the same bleached hair, albeit styled differently, and the same overly thin, hard countenance. But Jess recalled a warmth and kindness in Rhea's face that was completely absent in this woman, even at a glance. Beyond Tamra's mother and brother, the bar was virtually empty except for a couple at a corner table, talking quietly.

Jess waited for Tamra to make the next move. It was obvious they'd entered undetected, but he wondered if she would take advantage of the situation to keep putting off the encounter.

"You okay?" he whispered.

"For the moment," she whispered back. "It's just . . . amazing how the years can fly, and yet when I come back here it is as if I'd never been gone at all."

"You worked here, eh?"

"I probably spent more hours here than I ever spent in school," she said and took a deep breath. "Okay, here goes."

Jess squeezed her hand reassuringly just before she took a few more steps toward the bar and said in normal voice, "Hello, Mother."

Both heads turned abruptly toward them, and Jess could almost feel Tamra's heart pounding. Everything seemed to freeze for a long moment while Jess waited for some kind of reaction. Tamra's brother finally said, "Well, if it isn't the little vagabond."

"Is that really you?" Tamra's mother asked in a voice that grated with a lifetime of smoking and drinking. But she almost sounded pleased.

"It's me," Tamra said, her voice trembling slightly.

"Well, I hope you didn't come home because you need money. You won't get any from me."

"I don't need money, Mother," Tamra said.

"Then why *did* you come home?" she asked.

"I just came to see how you're doing, and I was hoping you might want to know how I'm doing. We won't keep you long, but . . . I was hoping we could just . . . talk for a few minutes."

Jess watched this woman's eyes as they shifted to him with stark appraisal. "And who is this?" she asked and took a long drag on her cigarette, blowing the smoke out slowly.

"This is Jess Hamilton," Tamra said, "my fiancé."

"Really?" she said, exactly as Tamra would have.

"Jess," Tamra went on, "this is my mother, Myrna, and my brother, Mel."

"It's a pleasure to finally meet you," Jess said.

"Oh, an Aussie," Myrna said, her tone caustic. She might as well have said, *Oh, a leper.* "My sister married an Aussie," she added, as if it had been tantamount to joining a terrorist organization.

"Best thing she ever did," Tamra countered, squeezing Jess's hand.

Following a tense minute of silence, Myrna motioned toward a table and said, "So, let's talk."

"Can I get you a drink?" Mel asked Tamra as Myrna sat at the table closest to the bar.

"No, thanks," she said.

"Still sticking to the Mormon nondrinking rule?" he asked, sounding only slightly snide. Tamra made no comment. Mel turned to Jess and asked, "How about you? Can I get you a drink? It's on me."

"I'll take a ginger ale, and so will she," he said.

Mel looked insulted and said, "I'll see if I can dig some up."

Jess coolly said, "Surely you have selections on hand for the designated drivers."

Mel ignored the comment and picked up a bottle of ginger ale that was within arm's reach. He poured out two glasses on ice and passed them over the bar. "Thank you," Jess said and followed Tamra to the table where her mother was sitting. He had a feeling this could get really interesting.

Chapter Two

"So, what have you been up to?" Myrna asked.

Tamra gave a succinct explanation of what she'd done since her mission, ending with the statement, "And now I'm getting married."

"So I see," Myrna said, glancing at Tamra's ring on the hand that held her glass. Then she glanced pointedly at Jess. "And what brings you here . . . all the way from Australia?"

"We came to see you," Tamra said.

Myrna's thickly penciled brows raised dramatically. "All the way from Australia?"

"That's right," Tamra said.

"You couldn't pick up a phone?"

"I wasn't sure you wouldn't hang up on me."

"Well, I might have," Myrna said.

"But you can't kick me out of a public establishment unless I engage in disorderly conduct. So, here I am."

"Yes, here you are," she said, as if she didn't trust Tamra's motives. "Are you sure you don't need money?" she asked, stamping out her cigarette in an ashtray on the table. "Cause if you do, you're wasting your time. Even if I had it I wouldn't give it to you."

"I'm sure," Tamra said.

As if to verify her suspicion of Tamra's motives, she asked Jess, "And what exactly do you do, Mr. Hamilton?"

"My family runs a horse station and a boys' home. The profit from one pretty much supports the other. I just do whatever needs to be done when I'm around."

"Did you go to school?"

"Off and on. I'm finishing up my degree via the Internet at the moment."

He expected her to ask what his major might be, but education didn't seem to be much of an interest beyond knowing that he had some. She leaned back and said, "Australia, huh. I can't see the appeal. It's just so . . . dry and desolate."

"Desert, kangaroos, and half-naked aborigines," Jess said with a sarcasm too subtle for anyone but Tamra to pick up on; her slight smile let him know that she had. "Yep, that's us," he added.

Myrna looked at him as if he'd just sprouted alien antennae. Mel approached, handed his mother a drink and sat beside her, cradling his own glass of what Jess guessed to be Scotch.

"I have some pictures," Tamra said, reaching into her purse.

"You do?" Jess asked. He couldn't recall ever seeing her with a camera.

While Tamra showed them pictures of his family, the house, the stables, the track, the yard, the boys' home, he saw the growing amazement in their eyes. She also had pictures of Rhea and her home, and some from her mission.

"And who is this?" Mel asked, pointing to the little girl with reddish-blonde hair.

"That's my brother's daughter, Evelyn," Jess said with obvious affection in his voice. "Her parents were killed in an accident when she was a baby."

While Myrna and Mel seemed only mildly interested, Tamra was amazed at the ease with which Jess made this statement. There had been a time when he could hardly look at Evelyn, let alone talk about the accident, without becoming upset.

"She's three," he added, "and absolutely adorable." Tamra met Jess's eyes, and for a moment her surroundings evaporated. Her mind went to their conversation on the plane, following his proposal of marriage, when he had told her he believed they should adopt Evelyn and raise her as their own. He believed it was what his brother wanted him to do, and Tamra couldn't deny that she instinctively agreed. She'd become very close to Evelyn while living in the Hamilton home and helping care for her. She suddenly missed the child very much, and looked forward to being with her again.

"She *is* cute," Myrna said in a voice that was only subtly patronizing. Jess and Tamra were both startled back to the moment and continued looking through the pictures.

When they were finally put away, Myrna looked at Jess as if she were seeing him differently. Recalling Tamra's explanation of her mother's priorities, Jess could almost hear her thinking, *Hmm, handsome* and *rich*. He hoped Tamra wouldn't hate him for saying the thought that wouldn't leave his mind. The awkward silence helped prompt him to it more easily. "I'm glad you clarified that thing about money." Myrna looked alarmed, almost guilty. "I mean, what you said about not giving money to family, even if you had it to give. Because I feel exactly the same way. Money just messes up family relationships, don't you think?"

Myrna's guilty eyes quickly became angry. Jess just smiled and tossed a quick glance toward Tamra, relieved to see the blatant approval in her eyes.

"So," Tamra said, "what have you been up to since we last talked?"

"Same old thing," Myrna said. "Nothing much changes around here."

They talked casually for a few more minutes before Myrna lit up another cigarette. Some customers came to the bar and Mel, who had hardly uttered a word in the conversation, got up to help them.

"Well, I guess we should be going," Tamra said. "It'll be getting pretty busy here soon."

Jess expected Myrna to say something to indicate that it had been nice seeing her daughter after all these years, but she glanced toward Jess with something akin to jealousy showing in her eyes as she said, "I must admit you got a fine catch here. Dare I say I'm surprised?"

"Of course you would be surprised," Tamra said, her voice firm, with just a hint of annoyance around its edges. "You made it clear many times that you never expected me to amount to much of anything. And yes, Jess is a fine catch," she added as if he weren't there. "But not for the reasons I know you're thinking."

"And how do you know what I'm thinking?" Myrna asked, seeming more amused than anything.

"I know you, Mother. If a man is handsome and rich, that's all that matters."

"Well," Myrna shrugged and motioned toward Jess with her cigarette, "he *is* handsome and rich. What more could you possibly ask for?"

"Yes, Mother," Tamra said, her voice a study in controlled anger, "he's rich and he's handsome—two facts which have absolutely nothing to do with my reasons for marrying him. I have a long list of qualifications, and he fits every one of them. Things like respect and commitment and spirituality. He works hard. He doesn't drink or smoke or do drugs. And he loves me. He has all the makings of a good husband and a good father. He was raised with supreme examples of love and respect in his home, and he's willing to marry me even though I wasn't. We will not scream at each other or our children. We will not abuse them or allow them to be abused. He is the only man I will ever marry, because we will do whatever it takes to make it last. And he is the only man I will ever let into my bed."

Myrna said nothing, but something vaguely humble showed in her eyes before she turned them shamefully downward. "Well," she said, rising to her feet, "I must admit it's been good to see you."

"Thank you," Tamra said. Jess stood beside her as she came to her feet as well. "It's good to see you, too. We'll keep in touch—if that's all right."

"Fine," Myrna said, as if she didn't care. "I assume the wedding will be in Australia."

"Yes, it will be," Tamra said. "We'll send pictures."

They exchanged cursory good-byes without so much as a handshake, let alone an embrace. Once they were out the door, Jess figured Tamra could probably use a hug, so he stopped on the sidewalk and pulled her into his arms. She clutched onto him tightly and he asked, "You okay?"

"I don't know," she said. "I have to think about it."

They got into the car before she said, "I'm hungry. How about you?"

"Yeah," he said.

"So, you find someplace to eat and I'll think."

"Whatever you wish, my lady," he said and she gave him a wan smile.

Jess pulled into the parking lot of a restaurant, then turned in his seat to face Tamra. "Want to talk about it?" he asked.

She looked toward him but said nothing. Wondering if she had cause to be unhappy with him, he just came out and asked, "Did I blow it, Tamra?"

She looked genuinely shocked. "No, of course not."

"Are you sure? Because I admit I was a bit obnoxious with them, and—"

"Which is exactly what you have to be to handle them; and you handled them beautifully, Jess." She showed a genuine smile. "You were superb, if you must know." Her eyes saddened and she turned them down. "I only wish I could stand up to them that way. I walked in there and felt like a little girl all over again. And I just—"

"Wait a minute," he said. "You were great in there, Tamra. And I'm not saying that just to make you feel better. As I see it, you did exactly what you came here to do. You made it clear that you aren't hanging onto the rift between you. You shared with her what you've done with your life, and you stood up to her. And you did it just like you told me you wanted to. You acted appropriately, and not at all angry and immature. I was proud of you in there, Tamra. It's one thing to stand up to someone you're indifferent toward. It's quite another to do it when you have so many emotional ties involved." He touched her face. "You did beautifully."

"You really mean that?" she asked, as if she didn't quite believe him.

"I really do," he said and she inhaled deeply. Her eyes grew distant and he gave her a few minutes to collect her thoughts. She finally smiled and said, "I think you're right. I *did* accomplish what I came here to do. And all things considered, it really couldn't have gone any better. Now I can at least write to her and not wonder if she'll throw the letters away."

"Would she do that?"

"She told Rhea in letters more than once to let me know that writing was a waste of time because she wasn't going to even open them. I sent several letters, during my mission and afterward."

For Tamra's sake, Jess suppressed his anger and said, "So, you've made some progress. Now you know you've done all you can do."

Tamra nodded, wondering why she still felt so uneasy when she expected to feel relieved. Not wanting to analyze it, she simply said, "Let's go eat. I'm starving."

After they were seated and had ordered, Tamra chuckled for no apparent reason.

"What's funny?" he asked.

"You were great back there," she said and lowered her voice to mimic him. "Desert, kangaroos, half-naked aborigines; yep, that's us."

Jess chuckled. "I've spent a lot of time in this country. And it amazes me how many people have such a limited impression of Australia."

"Well, my mother and brother just got a good lesson in *real* Australian culture."

"With pictures," he said and leaned over the table to kiss her.

They returned to the motel late in the afternoon, where Tamra said, "I am suddenly exhausted. Maybe it's jet lag."

"Could be," he said, walking toward their rooms. "Why don't you take a nap?"

"What about you?" she asked.

"I'm going to make a few phone calls, and then I'm going to take a nap too."

"Who are you going to call?" she asked.

"My parents, for one thing. I can actually call them now and not wake them up. And then I thought I'd get some plane reservations."

"Oh yeah, I forgot about that."

"Which reminds me," he said. "Are you in any hurry to get back?"

"Not especially, why?"

"I was thinking about stopping in Utah on our way back."

"Really?" she said with a delighted little laugh. "Can we go to Temple Square? I've dreamed of going there."

"I was planning on it. And I left some of my things there when I went home in a hurry. I'd like to pick them up and ship them back. I thought we could visit a few people, as well."

"Your sisters?" she said eagerly, recalling that Allison lived in Utah with her husband, Ammon, and their five children. And Emma, the youngest in Jess's family, was living with her sister, attending BYU.

"Of course, and a few other people." He grinned. "I want to show you off."

She smiled. "It sounds divine."

"Good," he said, "I'll arrange it." He opened her door and kissed her, saying, "Get some sleep and I'll see you in a few hours."

Jess enjoyed a good visit with his parents, telling them more about the changes that had taken place in his life. He felt closer to them than he ever had, and told them more than once how grateful he was to come from such an incredible heritage. He briefly described their visit with Tamra's mother, a situation that deepened his gratitude for his own family. They chatted a little about plans for the wedding, leaving Jess with a peaceful anticipation.

Jess called a travel agent and arranged the remainder of their journey. Tamra and Jess would work their way back home with stops in Utah and California. Then he fell asleep in the midst of silently thanking God for blessing his life so abundantly.

* * *

Once alone, Tamra felt a dark cloud descend upon her. It had hovered, barely at bay, since she'd first arrived in the city. But now it refused to be held back any longer. The city itself had stirred many memories—most of them unpleasant. But returning to the bar where she had spent uncounted hours of her life had been like stepping back in time. Having Jess with her had helped keep her distracted from the harsh realities of her upbringing. But now, in his absence, she could think of nothing beyond her reasons for leaving this place. Abuse, neglect, and lack of love all came marching through her mind like unwanted warriors invading a peaceful village.

Tamra experienced many hours of counseling in her youth. Joining the Church had helped her make leaps and bounds in her progress towards healing and putting the past behind her. But she'd always suspected that the emotional residue from her abuse was like a sleeping dragon that had yet to be fully confronted and conquered. And now she felt as if that dragon had been stirred. It was readily evident that the past wasn't nearly as far behind her as she'd wanted to believe. Lying in her motel-room bed, Tamra felt like a child all over again, fearing what kind of horror she might encounter with her mother's latest boyfriend or husband. Just seeing her mother's face earlier today had rekindled the debilitating anger she had once felt toward her mother. To this day, she could not understand how a woman could willingly ignore circumstances that were allowing her own children to be harmed.

For hours the memories marched on, luring Tamra further into a thickening darkness. She began to doubt the feelings that had urged her to make this visit, and with one doubt came another—and another. If she had been wrong about returning to Minneapolis, maybe she'd been wrong about many other decisions she'd made in her life. She couldn't question joining the Church or serving a mission. But beyond that, she had to wonder. Should she have gone to Australia? To stay with the Hamiltons? And what of Jess? Did she really know how to trust her feelings at all? Perhaps the decision to marry him was as wrong as her decision to be where she was now. Perhaps she was simply attracted to him and caught up with the idea of marrying into such an incredible family. It didn't take much effort to tally the vast differences between them—differences that could end up intruding on their happiness. Surely Jess Hamilton deserved better.

The doubt and confusion became so intense that Tamra felt as if her head would explode from the pressure. It was the thought of losing Jess that urged tears to the surface. Trickling over her face, they fell onto the pillow where she lay. With a box of tissues at her side, she cried harder and longer than she'd done since the childhood that had returned to haunt her.

Tamra finally slept while bizarre images of the past tainted her sleep. As she came slowly awake, she was reminded of emerging from a horrible fever she'd endured in the Philippines. It took her a minute to realize there was a lamp on. Knowing she hadn't left it on, she turned over abruptly and saw Jess sitting in a chair, his bare feet propped up on the edge of the bed.

"What are you doing here?" she asked through a yawn, recalling that they'd been given two keys to each room.

"Watching you sleep," he said. "I've already tried for nearly an hour to find something worth watching on TV; I had the sound down so I wouldn't wake you. So," he grinned, "I've been watching you."

"How quaint," she said, only slightly sarcastically. "I should have used the deadbolt. You never know who might break in."

"I did *not* break in," he said. "But yes, you probably should use the deadbolt." She said nothing and he added, "Looks like it's been snowing."

"It has?" she asked, lifting her head only to realize the drapes were closed.

"Well, I don't know about out there," he motioned idly toward the window, "but it's obviously been snowing in here." He nodded toward the floor and she peered over the edge of the bed to see dozens of used white tissues scattered over the carpet. She glanced guiltily toward him, only to have her fears confirmed. His expression made it clear that he expected an explanation. She closed her eyes, hoping he might let it drop, but he said in a voice that was gently demanding, "Do you want to tell me why you've been crying?"

"What makes you think I've been crying?" she asked tonelessly.

He ignored her effort to divert him and said, "You've been crying long and hard, and I want to know why."

"Well, I don't want to talk about it," she insisted, keeping her eyes closed.

Tamra expected him to adamantly counter her request, but she felt his fingers on her forehead and opened her eyes to see his face close to hers. In a gentle voice of compassion he said, "Maybe you should talk about it anyway." She said nothing and he added, "This is about your mother, isn't it?"

Tamra melted instantly into a fresh bout of tears. "Hey," he said, moving beside her. He leaned against the headboard and urged her to sit next to him, putting her head on his shoulder. "It's all right," he murmured, pressing a kiss into her hair.

"It doesn't feel all right," she said. "I thought I'd dealt with all of this years ago. I thought I'd become a mature, capable adult. But *no!*" she drawled then sniffled loudly. "I come home, take one look at my mother, and crumble like a child. All the . . . memories . . . and the feelings . . . just came at me like a freight train and I . . ." She became too emotional to speak, and Jess just let her cry, wishing he had any idea what he might say to console her.

After she had cried a few more minutes, he murmured quietly, "I know it feels horrible now, but we'll get through this, Tamra . . . together. We'll do whatever it takes."

She sprang to her feet so quickly it startled him. While she paced the room like a frightened animal, he felt an uneasy prickling at the back of his neck. After several minutes of watching her beat a path into the carpet, he broke the silence by saying firmly, "Talk to me, Tamra. You can't expect to deal with this in silence." Still she said nothing and he added, "You're the one who told me I needed to talk about my problems and—"

"Yeah, well maybe I was wrong," she snapped. "Maybe I was wrong about *everything!*"

Jess swallowed the temptation to get angry and forced away his growing fear. Maintaining a calm voice, he asked, "Do you want me to leave you alone?"

"Why don't you do that," she snarled. "In fact, why don't you go back to Australia and leave me here to just—"

"That's not what I meant," he countered.

"Well maybe it would be better if you did," she said without looking at him while her pacing became more vigorous. "Maybe you and I aren't as suited for each other as I was trying to make myself believe."

In one swift movement Jess took hold of her shoulders and forced her to face him. "Don't you dare even *think* such a thing after what we have been through! *You're* the one who told *me* that we were meant to be together, that what we shared was *destiny!*"

With hard eyes and a cold voice, she said, "Well, maybe it was just some . . . fantasy I came up with to justify making myself a part of your world. Maybe it would be better for you if we didn't go through with it."

Jess dropped his hands from her shoulders, unable to believe what he was hearing. While he was searching for some way to counter such a ridiculous statement, he looked down to see her pressing the ring into his hand that he'd given her earlier that day. Then she resumed her pacing, as if he weren't there. Engaging in silent prayer, he felt immeasurably grateful that he'd recently rediscovered the ability to communicate with his Father in Heaven. How could he possibly deal with something like this on his own? He tried to recall everything he knew about Tamra's upbringing. Early in their relationship, she had told him forthrightly that there had been some severe abuse in her childhood, but she'd gone on to tell him that she'd undergone a great deal of counseling, and when she had joined the Church she had been able to heal more deeply. She'd also told him that she feared suppressed memories of her abuse could very well come back to haunt her. Well, it was evident that they had, that she hadn't healed nearly as much as she'd believed. But hadn't she as much as admitted that very thing a few minutes ago? He felt surprisingly calm as it occurred to him that her perspective was presently distorted and he had to simply be loving and patient until she could come to terms with her past.

In a calm, firm voice he finally said, "Why don't you stop making irrational judgements and talk to me like a mature adult."

"Because I don't feel like a mature adult!"

"Okay . . . but you could at least stop walking and we can talk about this."

"What is there to say?" she insisted.

Jess took hold of Tamra's hand and urged her to sit on the edge of the bed. He sat close beside her and turned to face her, keeping her hand tightly in his, praying the Spirit would guide his words. "Now . . . don't get upset," he said. "Just . . . tell me why you are suddenly doubting something that you were so sure of before?" When she didn't answer he asked, "Have you . . . stopped loving me in the last couple of hours? Did you—"

"No, of course not," she said, looking at the floor.

"Then . . . what?" he asked gently.

She remained silent, but he sensed her mind working to come up with an answer and he waited patiently. She finally said, "It's just that . . . everything about you is so incredibly . . . wonderful. Your home, your family, your upbringing, and . . . you." She looked into his eyes and he felt relieved to see the obvious love and adoration that had always been there. "You're just such an incredible man, Jess. And suddenly this picture I have of our future seems so . . . impossible. And when I look at the reality of who and what I am, I don't know how it could possibly work."

Jess bit his tongue to stop from telling her exactly what he thought about that. After all they'd been through, he felt downright angry to hear her expressing feelings of unworthiness. Instead, he simply asked, "Why not?"

"Because . . . well . . . look at me. I was raised in a bar by an alcoholic mother and no father. I was abused by nearly every man she brought into her life and . . ." The coldness of her voice cracked with raw emotion. "And you're just such a . . . wonderful guy, and . . ."

"Oh," he said with subtle sarcasm, "would I be the same wonderful guy you left to rot in the psych ward because I'd taken twenty-five sleeping pills?"

Tamra looked completely astonished, as if she had momentarily forgotten that any such thing had ever happened. Before she could speak he went on, "I know you have some ugly things in your past, Tamra, and you certainly have the right to hurt over those things. But I think you're losing perspective here. Right now it's in your face. You've been confronted with a lot of memories and emotions today, but you're losing sight of the big picture. You rose above your upbringing and abuse. You went on a mission. You're an incredible woman. If not for you, I don't know if I ever would have been able to turn my own life around. I've told you before and I mean it as much now as I did then, you rose above the worst kind of upbringing to become a strong and amazing woman. I sank below the best kind of upbringing to become a loser. Do I have to remind you that I spent my youth in willful rebellion? That I smoked and drank and . . . worse?"

"But you're not a loser anymore, Jess. You've come beyond that."

"Yes, I have. And you've come beyond these pathetic circumstances you were raised in. You're an outstanding woman, and we are going to work this out and be extremely happy together."

Jess felt chilled by the disbelief in Tamra's eyes. Reminding himself of the advice he'd just given her, he attempted to keep his perspective. Following more silent prayer, he kissed her hand and said warmly, "I can understand why all of this is difficult for you, and the last thing I want you to do is brush it under the rug. You need to come to terms with it. If anything, I've become an expert on how you *don't* want to avoid coming to terms with the difficult things going on inside of you. But I think it has to come gradually, one step at a time, and I think you're too close to it—and too tired and hungry—to deal with it right now. What do you say we just . . . give it a little time, and we can talk about it whenever you want to. What do you say?"

He watched her take a deep breath before she lifted her eyes to look into his. They filled with fresh moisture, then she nodded stoutly and leaned her head on his shoulder. Jess sighed audibly and held her close, silently thanking God for helping them past that hurdle. He only prayed they could press on together and not let this come between them. He had to believe after all they had endured that they were meant to be together. It occurred to him that through his months of struggling to come to terms with his own heartaches,

Tamra had patiently and faithfully done her best to guide and strengthen him. Well, he would just have to do the same for her, no matter what it might take, no matter how long it might be.

"I love you, Tamra," he muttered, pressing his lips into her hair. "We'll get through this, together, I swear it."

"I love you too, Jess," she said, tightening her arms around him.

He sighed deeply then eased away enough to slide the ring back onto her finger. She looked briefly panicked and he hurried to say, "Until we're actually married, you have the option to call it off. All I ask is that you make certain fasting and prayer are a part of any such decision. In the meantime, I want you to wear this, and every time you look at it I want you to remember what I said when I gave it to you. That ring is a symbol of the love I feel for you; it means that you are worth everything I have, and everything I am—in spite of what your mother may have wanted you to believe."

Tamra sank into his arms and cried while he held her, feeling his heart break on her behalf. He wanted to go back to that bar and strangle her mother for bringing so much pain into her daughter's life. But he knew that nothing so childish would solve this problem.

When Tamra finally quieted down, he sensed the need for a distraction. "You know what we need?" he asked.

"A pizza?" she guessed just before her stomach growled audibly, provoking a chuckle from Jess.

"That's not what I was thinking," he said, "but it *is* a good idea."

"What were you thinking?"

"We need *music,* but the radio is just so . . . busy."

"I brought my laptop and some CDs," Tamra said.

"Really?" Jess said, then laughed, thinking how he'd started picking up the way Tamra frequently said that.

Tamra sat up and said, "I know that look in your eyes." He smiled, relieved to see that she was more like herself. "You want to *dance.*"

"How well you know me." He stood and held out his hand toward her. He helped her to her feet, gave her a quick kiss and said, "You fix the music; I'll order a pizza."

"It's a deal," she said.

They danced and laughed together for nearly two hours, stopping only now and then to feed each other pizza. Jess was grateful for the distraction that he hoped would help put things into perspective. But when exhaustion overcame them and they sat down to catch their breath, he saw that dark look come back into her eyes. Rather than ignoring it, he took her hand and said gently, "Tell me what you're thinking."

Tamra sighed, but at least she didn't argue. "I was just thinking how . . . I can't count the number of times in my life when I have tried to come up with one memory—just one—where I had some indication that my mother loved me. And I couldn't do it. Not one lousy memory."

Jess sighed and leaned his forearms on his thighs, pressing his fingers together. "I can't even begin to know how that feels," he said. "My parents always loved me—even when I was being an idiot." He looked over his shoulder at her. "But you know what? They love *you* too. And so do I. I'm not sure we can make up for all you've lost, but we're certainly going to try."

He saw that doubt rise into her eyes again and added, "You don't seem to believe me." She said nothing and he pressed, "Talk to me, Tamra. We can't get through this if you shut me out."

She sighed again. "Funny how I seem to recall saying similar things to you."

"Funny," he repeated with no hint of humor.

"Funny how I'm beginning to feel like a hypocrite."

"Only if you don't talk to me and let it come between us," he said.

"Okay, well . . . I have to admit that the love and acceptance I have gotten from you and your family is the best thing that's ever happened to me, with the exception of joining the Church. And I'm grateful for that; I truly am. It's just that . . . all things considered, the whole thing just seems so *surreal*. I feel like I'm in a fairy tale and I'm going to wake up because it's just too good to be true."

"It wasn't too good to be true yesterday," he said.

She looked pointedly away. "Well, maybe I lost sight of the real me, and maybe when you find out what I'm really like, you'll change your mind about marrying me and—"

"Or maybe," he interrupted, "what happened today made you lose sight of the real you, and it's the real you that I fell in love with."

Seeing a vague glimmer of hope in her eyes, he figured he'd get no better opportunity to say, "There's something I came to your room earlier to talk to you about, and then I found all that snow on the floor and . . . we got a little distracted."

"I'm listening," she said, as if it might be bad news.

"I talked to my parents for quite a while. They said to tell you they love you and miss you." He took a deep breath, wondering why something that had seemed so easy only hours ago had suddenly become difficult. "And . . . they were wondering how we'd feel about getting married soon after New Year's—when the temple reopens after the holidays. That way the family can come home for the holidays and be there for the wedding." When she said nothing, he felt the need to clarify, "I know you're having a rough time, Tamra, and like I said earlier, you have the option to call it off. But I hope you would only do so if you knew beyond any doubt that it's the right thing to do. My hope is that you'll put enough faith in me—in us—to press forward with our plans, believing that we can get through this and you can feel good about committing your life to me."

Tamra looked at the sadness mingled with hope in his eyes and couldn't deny that her deepest wish was to be his wife and become a part of the great legacy she had gotten a taste of while staying at his home in Australia. Instinctively she believed it was right. She simply had to get beyond these horrible doubts and know for certain that she would not be bringing unforeseen difficulties into *his* life from this pathetic baggage she was carrying. Until today, she had believed—or at least hoped—that the baggage was gone. But obviously it wasn't, and it scared her. Still, Jess was right. His love for her was evident, and she had to put her faith in him to help get her through this. Praying he wouldn't regret it, she put her hand into his and said, "That sounds perfect."

Jess wasn't sure if she meant the wedding date or his attitude about pressing forward. Either way, it was a step in the right direction. He kissed her quickly before they said good night and he returned to his room, but it was a long while before he finally fell asleep, praying with all his heart that they would get beyond this and find the happiness together that they'd just begun to enjoy.

* * *

Emotionally exhausted, Tamra fell quickly to sleep in spite of her long, late nap. She was awakened by the phone ringing and she groped for it in the dark. "Hello," she said groggily.

Jess's voice said with the excitement of a child, "Have you looked outside?"

"No, I haven't looked outside." She glanced at the clock. "It's not even five o'clock in the morning. It's still dark out there."

"Not exactly," he said. "Look outside, and I'll be over to get you in five minutes."

"What?" she asked, but he hung up the phone.

Tamra groaned and dragged herself toward the window, wondering if she could keep up with all of Jess's energy. She rubbed her eyes in hopes of making them focus better as she pulled back the heavy drapes, then gasped. She tried to remember if it had been snowing when Jess left her room last night, but she realized she'd been so tired that she hadn't even looked out. And now, everything was blanketed with perfect white. Snow clung to every tree and power line, and a nearly full moon had broken through the clouds, illuminating everything in its path with a pearly glow. The words from a famous Christmas story came to mind. *The moon on the breast of the new fallen snow gave a luster of midday to objects below.*

Fully awake with childlike excitement, Tamra scrambled to get dressed and put on her new boots and coat, delightfully oblivious to yesterday's drama. She was pulling on her gloves when Jess knocked quietly at her door. She opened it to see him dressed the same way, wearing the scarf and silly hat she had bought for him. She was thinking that she'd left both her hats in the car when he produced her silly one and pulled it snugly down over her ears. "All set," he said. "The car's warm. Let's go."

"Where are we going?" she asked as he took her hand and pulled the door shut.

"You'll see," was all he said.

Tamra wondered where they might be going, and was surprised when he stopped the car in front of the Walker Art Museum, which they had driven by yesterday. The moonlight clearly illuminated the sculpture garden of modern art as Jess led her by the hand to a particular spot where he announced firmly, "We are going to build a snowman!"

"Not here, you're not," she said and laughed.

"Is it illegal or something?" he asked, bending down to attempt scooping some snow together in his hands.

"No," she laughed again, "but I think you're accustomed to wet Utah snow. You can't pack this dry stuff together, no matter how hard you try."

After several attempts he finally had to admit she was right. Instead they ran and played tag like children, and made numerous snow angels. When she became too cold to enjoy this excursion any longer, they returned to the car. Jess hesitated before he opened the door for her, gazing at her tenderly. Tamra caught a glisten in his eyes and could almost guess his thoughts. She couldn't deny that getting some distance from all she'd been feeling last night had certainly helped her perspective. Her heart quickened as he impulsively kissed her. She became oblivious to her cold toes and fingers and nose as he enfolded her in his arms and kissed her again and again.

"Careful, Jess," she said, "if our lips freeze together, whoever comes to open this building will find us here and we could get arrested for kissing on public property."

"Is that illegal here?" he asked quite seriously.

"Not that I know of, but why take any chances?" She rubbed his nose with hers and said, "I love you, Mr. Hamilton."

"And I love you—Mrs. Hamilton-almost."

They returned to the motel room in the predawn light and watched the sun come up just before they went into their separate rooms to warm up and get a little more sleep before they were supposed to check out. It took Tamra a while to fall back to sleep as she contemplated all that had happened in the last twenty-four hours. Never in her life had she experienced such an emotional roller coaster. The lows had been horribly low, but at least she could be grateful that the highs had been such a stark contrast. She finally slept, holding onto the belief that Jess would keep his promise—that they would see this through, together.

Chapter Three

Once again the ringing phone brought Tamra awake. Jess's voice said, "Good morning, my love."

"Good morning," she replied.

"We're supposed to check out in less than an hour but—"

"Oh my gosh." She sat straight up. "I've got to hurry and—"

"Hold on there," he said. "Let me finish. I've already asked if we can keep the rooms."

"Keep them? Why?" she asked, wanting to get out of this city as quickly as possible.

"Well," he drawled, "I couldn't sleep . . . and I did a lot of praying and . . . I just feel like we need to stick around a few days. I've already canceled the flight reservations."

Tamra resisted the urge to yell at him. She forced a calm voice as she asked, "You could have asked me first."

"Yes, I could have. But I would have had to wake you up a long time ago to do that, and I couldn't wait too long or it would cost me more to . . . Never mind. That's not important. If you want to leave, I'll get another flight out as soon as possible. But . . . well, I was kind of hoping you'd show me around a little and maybe we could make some *good* memories here for you before we leave."

Tamra sighed. She felt what Jess was saying made sense, even though she didn't like it. She had to admit, "You mean like . . . playing in the snow in the middle of the night?"

"Yeah, like that," he said with a little chuckle.

"Okay . . . well, I guess this means I can go back to sleep for an hour."

"Yes, actually you can. Do you want to go out for breakfast when you get up? Or do you want me to go get something and bring it back?"

"I want to go out," she said. "In fact . . . I want bacon and hash browns, and there's this great place not far from the bar where . . ." She hesitated as something uneasy pricked at her.

As if he'd read her mind, Jess said, "New memories, Tamra. Go back to sleep. I'll see you in an hour."

When Tamra *couldn't* go back to sleep, she soaked in the bathtub for a short while and was completely ready to go when Jess called to wake her up. While they were sharing a huge breakfast, including what Jess called *the best hash browns on earth,* he said, "So, where should we go first?"

"Oh, we're going on the lake and river drive," she said. "It's beautiful; you'll love it."

"Okay," he said with a grin.

Before they finished eating, he said, "Tamra, I had another thought this morning that I just can't get rid of."

"I am *not* going back to that bar. There is no way you can—"

"And why do you think I would want you to do that? You're getting paranoid, my dear. I was simply going to ask if . . . Do you have any idea where your father is?"

Tamra was briefly stunned into silence. She finally admitted, "No."

He leaned over the table and asked, "Wouldn't you like to find out?"

"No," she said again and he scowled at her. "Listen, Jess. I barely remember him. I've only seen him twice in my life, and that was briefly, and many years ago. Do I really want to get to know a man that my mother would leave? Most of the creeps she had in her life actually left *her.* So, what kind of man would she want to be rid of?"

"He's still your father, Tamra. We're a long way from Australia. While you're here, you ought to at least try." He smiled and added, "I'll hold your hand."

Tamra blew out a long breath, unable to refute the feeling she had that he might be right. She'd always wondered about her father, and if nothing else, it might give her some kind of closure with him, as opposed to the floating uncertainty that had always been a part of her life.

"Okay, fine," she said. "We can try."

"That's my girl," Jess said.

Before they left the restaurant, Tamra looked carefully through the phone book but couldn't find him. "Do you know anyone who might know where he is?" Jess asked.

"Yes," she said with an edge to her voice. "My mother."

Their eyes met for a long moment before Jess asked, "Do you want *me* to call her?"

Tamra thought about it for a minute and said, "No, I can call her. I ought to be grown up enough to handle *that.*"

It took her a few minutes to gather the courage to punch out the bar's number from a pay phone. Mel answered the phone and Tamra quickly asked, "Is Myrna there?"

"Who's calling?" he asked gruffly.

"It's Tamra," she said firmly.

She could hear him putting a hand over the receiver to muffle his voice, then he came back and said, "She's busy."

"I'll only keep her half a minute," she said.

"I said she's busy."

"Okay, well . . . do you have any idea where I might find our father?"

Following a moment of silence, he said, "Why on earth would you want to find that good-for-nothing bum?" He hung up the phone before she could respond.

"That went well," Tamra said with sarcasm, slamming down the phone. "Maybe we should just . . . go to a museum or something."

"Okay," he said, "let's go."

They returned to the Walker Art Museum, this time going inside to enjoy the variety of modern art. Then they took the lake and river drive Tamra had mentioned earlier. It took them around all of the heavily forested city lakes, which were surrounded by neighborhoods of large older homes, then down to the Mississippi River by St. Anthony Falls and the locks. The trees were spectacular, glazed with ice and snow, and Jess commented many times that there was a great deal of beauty in this city. "After all," he added, "*you* were born here." Tamra only scowled at him. That evening they ate Chinese food in Jess's room while they watched an old movie, then they had a late-evening swim in the motel's indoor pool.

Lying in bed that night, Tamra tried to tell herself she was relieved that Jess had dropped the subject of finding her father, and the fact that her mother and brother had refused to cooperate. But she could hardly relax as speculations about what her father might be like floated through her mind. She wondered if seeing him might make her feel better or worse. She recognized this feeling of unrest, and she knew in her heart that she had to act on it. She simply had to do everything in her power to find her father.

Tamra slept late and woke to realize she was getting into some horrible habits. Late nights and late mornings were not what she was accustomed to. But considering how difficult it had been for her to sleep, she figured it was a blessing that she didn't have to get up and be anywhere. In truth, she hadn't had a vacation in a very long time. Or had she ever? And maybe once she got past trying to find her father, it might start to *feel* like a vacation. She shared her thoughts with Jess over a late breakfast and he heartily agreed. "You deserve a vacation, Tamra. And I'm going to see that you get one. After all, you worked very hard the last several months to get me back on my feet."

"And now you get to return the favor," she said with an irony that she knew he picked up on when their eyes met. He just reached across the table and squeezed her hand.

Following a drive downtown, Tamra couldn't believe she was actually walking back into the bar her mother owned. "They need to get out more," Jess whispered when they entered to see her mother and Mel sitting in exactly the same place they'd been at this time two days ago.

"Hello again," Tamra said, attempting to sound jovial.

They both turned in surprise before Myrna stamped out her cigarette with an angry air. "You can't honestly want to hunt down that no-good father of yours," she rumbled.

"I guess I don't have to ask if Mel told you I called," Tamra said.

When only silence followed, Jess asked, "Do you know where he is?"

Tamra was pleased to see that her mother seemed slightly intimidated by Jess. Myrna said snidely, "He's still in the city as far as I know. He married some bimbo, last I heard."

"Do you know where he was working?" Tamra asked.

"You really don't want to see him, girl," she said in a voice that was almost threatening. "I can assure you that you'll regret it."

"Okay, so I'll regret it. Do you know where he was working?"

"Rockbridge Construction," she said. "But that was years ago. I doubt the bum would keep a job this long." Myrna then went into a tirade about the horrible things Tamra's father had done, as if they were all Tamra's fault. When her language became increasingly colorful, Jess interrupted, saying brightly, "Oh, listen, Tam. They're playing our song." And then to her mother, "Thanks for your help. If you'll excuse us. It's our song."

He hurried her across the bar to an unoccupied corner and pulled her close as he eased her into a slow dance. "What are you doing?" she whispered. "Why don't we just leave?"

"And give them the pleasure of seeing us storm out? Of having the last word? No, this is better." He eased back and smiled at her. "New memories, Tamra."

Tamra marveled at his insight and wisdom. Oh, how she loved him! Looking into his eyes, she could almost forget the ugliness of her childhood that this place so fully represented.

"Our song, huh?" she asked, trying to tune into the music. "I don't think I've heard this song before in my life."

"Well, it's our song now," he said. "Just listen."

"Have you heard it before?"

"Yes, I have. Just listen."

Tamra tuned her ears to the sultry jazz music, but it took her a minute to grasp the lyrics being repeated in the chorus. *There's nothing like you and I . . . This is no ordinary love, no ordinary love.* Before the song ended, Jess urged her into a dizzying spin, and then a flamboyant dip. She laughed as she regained her equilibrium, then he hurried her toward the door, waving comically toward Myrna and Mel, who were both staring with incredulous expressions. "Bye," Tamra said, then heard herself giggle as they came into the open air.

"Thank you," she said, pausing to hug Jess tightly.

"For what?" he asked with a laugh.

"You just have a way of . . . making everything better."

"And all this time I thought it was *you* making everything better."

In the car, Tamra's mood soured with thoughts of her mother. She growled involuntarily and Jess said, "Stop thinking about her. You never have to see her again if you don't want to."

"That's somewhat of a relief," she said. "But . . . do you have any idea how it feels to know I'm the *offspring* of such a person?"

He offered her a compassionate glance and squeezed her hand. "No, I don't," he said. "But I've told you before, Tamra my love, you're the cream of the crop."

"Yes, well . . . if the crop's all bad, how good can the cream be?"

"In this case, it's sweet and fine . . . and adorable."

They went back to the motel where Tamra called Rockbridge Construction and asked the woman who answered, "Do you have a Brady Banks working for you?"

The woman kindly asked, "May I ask who wants to know?"

Tamra felt a small surge of hope at the woman's question, and it surprised her to realize how badly she wanted to find her father. "This is his daughter. I'm in the country for just a short time and was hoping to see him, but it's been years and—"

The woman interrupted and said, "He's the supervisor on the Davenport project."

Tamra's heart quickened. "And . . . what exactly is that?" she asked.

"New hotel going in, in downtown St. Paul."

"Thank you," she said, then as an afterthought, she quickly added, "Could I leave the number of where I'm staying? If I miss him, could you have him call me?"

"Sure," the woman said, and Tamra gave her the information.

"Thank you very much," Tamra said and got off the phone. She looked at Jess and took a deep breath. "He's supervising a new hotel being built in downtown St. Paul. She gave me the address."

Driving toward the other Twin City, Tamra had to admit, "I'm really nervous, Jess. I don't even remember how old I was the last time I saw him. All I really remember is him arguing with my mother and leaving angry. I doubt I'd know him if I saw him and . . . oh, my gosh. There it is." With the huge cranes towering above the surrounding buildings, it was easy to spot the new hotel going up. Jess drove around the construction site twice before he found a suitable place to park across the street from what looked like a main entrance. They approached a man there and Jess asked, "We're looking for Brady Banks. Is he—"

"I'm not sure where he is," the man said in an annoyed voice. "And you can't go any further without a hard hat and an employee pass."

"I really need to see him," Tamra said, certain her nerves could never tolerate waiting another day.

"And who are you?" he asked.

"An old friend," Tamra said impulsively. "I'd just like to see him for a minute, if that is at all possible."

The man pulled a cell phone from a clip on his belt and punched in a number. In a respectful tone that in no way resembled how he'd spoken to them, he said, "There's someone here to see you; says she's an old friend." Following some silence while he was obviously listening, he said, "Okay, I'll tell her."

Tamra's heart pounded as the man turned off his phone before he said, "He'll be down in a minute. He said you should wait inside." He led them inside what would obviously be the lobby of the hotel. It was only slightly warmer than outside.

The man walked away and Tamra shivered visibly. "Cold?" Jess asked.

"Yes, and scared to death."

"It's not *that* bad."

"As I recall, Jess Hamilton, you weren't terribly thrilled to see your parents not so long ago."

Jess blew out a long breath. Following his suicide attempt, seeing his parents had been one of the most difficult things he'd ever faced. "Okay, you got me there," he said. "I have no idea how you feel, so I'll just stop trying to guess."

"It's okay, Jess," she said. "I just . . ." She stopped when she saw a man approaching. From a distance he looked vaguely familiar, but across the front of his hard hat it distinctly said *Banks*.

Before he got too close, Tamra turned her back to him abruptly and whispered to Jess, "What if he doesn't want anything to do with me? What if he's mean to me? What will I do?"

"Then you'll know you tried, and we'll go home and put it behind us. Turn around and get it over with."

Tamra turned around and took advantage of the opportunity to get a good look at her father as he approached. He looked a little taller and broader than Jess; his face looked younger than she had expected. He wore jeans and work boots. His jacket hung open to reveal a dark-colored button-up shirt with a tie. He looked well groomed and sharp, and she felt surprised by the overall impression. If it wasn't for the name on the hard hat, she'd think for sure they had the wrong man. Jess whispered with gentle sarcasm, "He looks like a real loser, Tamra."

Tamra watched as her father approached the guy they'd talked to, and he pointed toward her and Jess. Her father looked skeptical, obviously knowing these people weren't *friends*. He approached them and said, "I'm Brady Banks. Can I help you?"

Tamra almost wondered if this could possibly be the man she'd always believed to be the loser her mother had described. She was searching for the right words to ask when he pulled off his hat and pushed a hand through his reddish hair. She was grateful that Jess picked up on her inability to speak when he said, "It's a pleasure to meet you, Mr. Banks." He extended a hand, which Brady shook heartily, albeit still looking confused.

"And you would be . . ." Brady asked.

"Jess Hamilton . . . the man who is going to marry your daughter."

Brady turned startled eyes toward Tamra. They narrowed, then widened, then sparkled when he smiled. "Tamra?" he asked with tender trepidation.

"Hello, Dad," she said. He caught his breath and embraced her tightly.

"I can't believe it," he said, pulling back to look at her face closely while he held her shoulders. "I haven't seen you since you were a little girl. You've grown up, and you're so beautiful."

Tamra looked up into her father's face, overcome with an enormous mixture of emotions. She finally found her voice enough to utter, "I . . . don't know what to say."

Brady Banks chuckled and hugged her again, then glanced at his watch. "I hate it," he said, "but I've got to get back to work. I've got an inspector coming but . . . I'd love to see you later. There's so much I want to say . . . so much to catch up on. Could I treat the two of you to dinner? Do you have plans, or—"

"We'd love to," Jess answered for Tamra.

"Great," Brady said.

"Would you like us to meet you somewhere, or—"

"That would be great," Brady grinned. "How about the Top of the Radisson at 6:30?"

"We'll be there," Jess said.

"It's at—"

"I know where it is," Tamra said and Brady chuckled again, as if her appearance had made him the happiest man in the world.

In the car, Tamra could only say, "I can't believe it. I just can't believe it. He's nothing like I remember . . . or even imagined. Do you think he's changed that much? Or are my memories just totally distorted?"

"Or maybe," Jess said, "your mother tainted the picture because she didn't *want* you to like him."

Tamra really liked that idea, but she couldn't hide the cynicism in her voice as she said, "Or maybe he just gives a really great first impression, and it takes time to realize he's a dysfunctional jerk."

"Well, then." Jess smiled. "I guess we'll just have to give it a little time."

"Or maybe we should just keep it brief and I can enjoy believing he's a nice guy."

Jess tossed her a cautious glance. "If you don't get to know him, you might be missing out on something that could make a positive difference in your life."

"Or a negative one," she insisted.

Jess pulled into the motel parking lot and put the car into park before he turned to face her and said, "Listen, Tamra. This is your family, your issues. I'm just here to hold your hand. But he really seems like a nice guy, and you can't question that he was glad to see you."

Tamra turned away from him and said, "Why does *a nice guy* leave his children to be raised by a woman like my mother?"

Jess sighed and took her hand. "I don't know, Tamra. Maybe you should ask him."

Tamra couldn't acknowledge what Jess had said; she didn't even want to think about it. But through the remainder of the day, she thought of nothing else. She felt startled by the impression she'd gotten of her father earlier that day, and disconcerted by trying to fit this man into the picture her mother had painted of him. Insisting she needed some rest before they went out to dinner, Tamra curled up in her bed and attempted to pray away her nervousness. By the time Jess came to get her to keep their appointment, she knew that, one way or another, she could not leave Minneapolis without at least trying to understand this man who had had so much impact on her life—even in his absence, or maybe *especially* by his absence. The only solution was to spend some time with him, and yes, perhaps just come right out and ask him about his choice to be severed from her life.

"You okay?" Jess asked while driving toward the Radisson.

"Just thinking," she said and he left her to it. On their way up in the elevator, she pressed both hands over her middle, as if she could quell the hovering butterflies.

"Don't think too hard," Jess suggested. "Just let the evening . . . happen; go with your feelings, and you can think about it later."

Tamra nodded bravely, liking that advice. "Okay, let's go," she said. Jess took her hand as the elevator door opened and she added, "I really like having you around to hold my hand."

"The feeling is mutual," he said. "Besides . . . I'm still deeply indebted on that count. You're going to have to go through a lot more trauma than this before I could ever get even."

"You don't need trauma as an excuse to hold my hand," she said.

He grinned and kissed her quickly before they stepped into the restaurant.

A hostess approached them and Jess said, "We were supposed to meet a Mr. Banks here, and—"

"He's already here," she said. "Come this way."

They were led between many tables where people were eating and talking. Tamra's heart quickened when she saw her father. Seated beside him was a woman with blonde hair that had more fluff than curl, and that hung past her shoulders. They both came to their feet when the hostess motioned Jess and Tamra to the table. "Ah, there you are," Brady said, taking both Tamra's hands and kissing her on the cheek. He shook Jess's hand. "It's good to see you again, Mr. Hamilton."

"And you," Jess said.

Brady turned toward the woman and said, "I'd like you to meet my wife, Claudia. Claudia, this is my daughter, Tamra, and her fiancé. . . Jess, isn't it?"

"That's right," Jess said.

"It's so good to meet you," Claudia said with sincerity. She smiled brightly, showing straight, white teeth between rusty colored lips. Tamra noticed that her skin looked like an old woman's, as if it had aged prematurely from a life spent in the sun, a stark contrast to the youthful aura about her, and the brilliant sparkle in her eyes. "When Brady called to tell me that you'd shown up, I thought he was just going to burst with happiness."

Brady beamed in response to her comment. "It's a pleasure to meet you as well," Tamra said, and they were all seated.

"There's so much to choose from," Claudia said. "We should likely be looking over the menu." They all fell into silence, but it didn't feel uncomfortable as they became absorbed in the choices of food available.

"Would you like to see the wine list?" Brady asked Tamra, setting his hand over a smaller menu lying on the table.

"No, thank you," she said. "We don't drink."

"Well, that gives us something in common," he said with a warm smile. "I reached a point where I realized the only way to stop drinking too much was to stop drinking at all."

Tamra exchanged a discreet glance with Jess, certain he'd picked up on this possible clue to changes in Brady Banks's life. Once they had ordered, Brady leaned his forearms on the table and looked at Tamra as if he'd never seen anything so amazing in his life. "So, tell me about yourself, Tamra," he said. "I want to know everything."

Tamra laughed tensely and glanced down, grateful to feel Jess reaching for her hand. "I hardly know where to begin . . . or what to say."

"Well, you're getting married. That's wonderful. Tell us how you and Jess met. That's a good place to start."

Tamra felt awkward at first as she told him of going to the Philippines to serve a mission, which required an explanation of her joining the Church. They listened with interest, and while Brady readily admitted that religion had never been a part of his life, he believed in God, and he respected her for making such choices. With that out of the way, she began to relax as they ate bread and salad and she told them of her reasons for going to Australia to live with her mother's sister, Rhea, for a couple of years, and how she had eventually felt compelled to go and stay with the Hamiltons. She said nothing of the struggles they had been through during the past several months; she simply told them, "I think Jess and I practically fell in love at first sight, but it took a while to get life sorted out."

"Well, I can certainly relate to that," Brady said, exchanging a tender glance with Claudia.

"So, now it's your turn," Jess said. "Tell us how the two of you met."

Brady looked only slightly tense for a moment before he said, "I hope you won't think any less of me for admitting that we met at an Alcoholics Anonymous meeting."

"Of course not," Tamra said.

"Far better there than at some sleazy bar," Claudia said, squeezing Brady's hand where it rested on the table.

"Well said," Jess interjected.

"Anyway," Brady passed his wife an adoring glance that reminded Tamra of the way Jess's parents looked at each other, "Claudia was a lot further ahead in the game; it was my first meeting. But we looked at each other and . . . everything just kind of changed. She helped me get through some pretty tough weeks, and given some time, we realized our lives would be better spent together." He looked more at Jess and Tamra as he added, "Claudia's got three great kids. They were all teenagers when we got married—over nine years ago. They're all on their own now. We even have a little grandson."

"That's great," Tamra said and Claudia pulled pictures from her wallet, which they passed around and admired. Tamra couldn't help noticing the pride Brady felt in discussing Claudia's family as if they were his own. She thought of the fact that Jess had three half-sisters, and how completely his father had taken them in as his own after their mother's first husband had been killed. That's the way it should be, she concluded. But she didn't like being such a stranger to her own father, when he was so involved in the lives of his stepchildren.

After they had settled into their main course, Tamra pulled the same pictures out of her purse that she had shown to her mother. But Brady and Claudia showed a great deal more interest and enthusiasm over seeing where she and Jess lived and worked. They asked many questions about Australia and Jess's family. And she was surprised to hear Jess telling them a great deal about Evelyn, and how they intended to adopt her. He mentioned that her parents had been killed, but offered no further explanation. Still, to see him mention it so comfortably gave Tamra hope that she could eventually get beyond her own struggles. She hesitated over a picture of Evelyn, wondering how she was doing. Did Evelyn miss her as much as she missed Evelyn?

Pictures from the Philippines elicited more questions over Tamra's mission. The conversation was comfortable and pleasant, while Tamra felt almost as if she were dreaming. Could this really be her *father?* There was so much she wanted to ask him, so much she needed to know. But over dinner in a crowded restaurant was not the time or place to bring up sensitive family issues. She reminded herself to heed Jess's advice. *Just let the evening happen, go with your feelings, and you can think about it later.*

Brady insisted on paying for the meal, but Jess insisted on paying the tip. Unlike her mother, her father didn't seem to have taken any notice of the evidence he'd seen in several photographs of the obvious affluence in Jess's family.

As they stood up from the table, Brady asked, "Are you two in a hurry to get anywhere?"

Jess turned to Tamra, obviously giving her the option to continue their time together, or draw it to a close. She appreciated his sensitivity, but she eagerly said, "No, we're on vacation. Did you have something in mind?"

"Well," Brady said, "I hate to let you go when we're just getting acquainted. Maybe you could follow us to the house and we could visit some more or—"

"Brady, honey," Claudia said, "weren't you going to stop and—"

"Oh, that's right," he said. "We do have to make a stop on the way—just a quick visit." He grinned. "But it is someone I think you'd like to meet. What do you say?"

"We'll just follow you," Jess said.

When Jess and Tamra were alone in the car, following the dark-colored SUV that Brady was driving, Jess asked, "How you doing so far?"

"Fine . . . I think," she said. "I'm just a little . . . amazed. They're such good people. I don't sense any phoniness from them at all. It just doesn't fit with what I've always believed."

"Well, he as much as admitted to some big changes in his life. I really think you should just ask him."

"Yes, I think so too, but . . . it's not an easy thing to get around to. I'm hoping—no *praying*—for the right moment."

"And it doesn't have to be tonight," Jess said. "We can see them again, you know. So just go with your feelings, okay?"

"Okay," she said, squeezing his hand.

After following the other vehicle for nearly half an hour, they pulled up in front of a convalescent center. "Someone he'd like you to meet, huh?" Jess said as he turned off the engine.

Tamra made no comment. She felt a subtle jittery feeling deep inside, not unlike what she'd felt earlier when she'd faced her father— but somehow she also felt more tranquil. They met up with Brady and Claudia on the front walk and Tamra asked, "So who are we visiting?"

"My mother," Brady said, putting an arm around Tamra's shoulders as they walked.

But Tamra stopped abruptly and he had no choice but to do the same. In a voice that quavered, she asked, "I have a grandmother?"

"You do," Brady said, and Tamra watched as her father's image became blurred because of the tears that rose in her eyes. Her mother's parents had both died in her early childhood. And in spite of the connections she felt to Jess's family, he had no grandparents living. Tamra recalled hearing friends tell of visits to a grandparent's home, and how she'd dreamed of having a tender family connection that crossed more than one generation. While she tried to put together a coherent response, Brady added, "She had a stroke a couple of years ago, and we just weren't able to take care of her on our own any longer. I'm sure she'll be tickled to see you again."

"Again?" Tamra echoed, unable to recall any such meeting.

"Well, she hasn't seen you since you were just two or three, I'd guess; that's about when the divorce happened." Brady briefly touched Tamra's hair. "You have her to thank for this beautiful red hair, although hers has gone silver now."

"In that case," Jess said, "I must thank her, as well. I don't think there is hair this beautiful in all the world."

"Amen," Brady said and they went into the building.

Chapter Four

Just inside the door of the care center was a little office with a big, open window, where a thin, middle-aged woman sat at a desk. She looked up at the sound of the door, then smiled, "Hello there. I suspected you'd show up sooner or later."

"How are you, Pam?" Claudia asked, reaching through the window to take the woman's hand. "Has your knee been giving you any more trouble?"

"It's doing a little better, actually," Pam said.

Her eyes turned to Jess and Tamra just as Brady said, "Pam, I'd like you to meet my daughter, Tamra, and her fiancé, Jess Hamilton."

They exchanged greetings before Pam said to Brady, "Is this the daughter you've been wondering about all this time?"

"She's the one," Brady said, smiling toward Tamra.

She wanted to question him on that, but Pam went on to say, "Rayna is probably still in the cafeteria."

"That's what I suspected," Brady said. "She does like to sit in there where the action is."

Pam went back to her work and they turned the corner and went down a long hall, past a number of rooms where the open doors showed elderly people watching television or resting. Her heart quickened at the thought of meeting her grandmother, but she also felt a sense of dread as she wondered what condition she might be in. She didn't even know this woman, but already her heart ached for her. A stroke. She wished she had any idea what to expect.

As they entered the cafeteria, Tamra saw that the room looked as if it served many purposes. There was a television playing in one corner, with some chairs gathered around it, all occupied. There were a few games of chess and checkers in progress. Many of the occupants of the room were in wheelchairs, or had walkers nearby. Tamra became briefly distracted by the varying degrees of disability that represented the difficulty of growing old. She was startled to hear Claudia say with genuine affection, "Hello, dear. I miss you when we can't get here every day."

Tamra wondered if this was her grandmother or just another patron they'd gotten to know. But her father squatted beside the same woman, saying, "There you are, Mom. You're looking pretty tonight."

Rayna Banks, a long, thin woman with short, silvery hair was seated in a wheelchair. She was dressed in a pink jogging suit, with white canvas shoes on her feet. A watch on a chain hung around her neck and she wore wedding rings. Recognition showed in the old woman's eyes as Brady spoke to her, but she made no response.

Brady took his mother's frail hands into his and said, with happiness in his voice, "Mama, I've brought someone to see you, someone very special." Tamra felt the old woman's eyes shift away from her son, but they didn't focus on Tamra until she moved closer and sat on a chair near her father. "Mother," he said, putting his arm around Tamra's shoulders, "this is my little girl, Tamra. It's been more than twenty years since you've seen her. Do you remember?"

Tamra looked into her grandmother's eyes and caught a definite sparkle, although she couldn't determine if it was recognition or inquisitiveness. Following her father's example, Tamra took her grandmother's hand, saying, "I'm sorry I don't remember you, Grandma, but I can't tell you how it thrills me to see you now."

Rayna's eyes smiled brilliantly and Tamra was assaulted with emotion that she fought to keep in check. *Her grandmother!* It was a miracle. She briefly pondered all the genealogy she had done for her ancestors, and she wondered why the name Rayna didn't sound familiar, or why she had failed to realize that she had a living grandmother. Perhaps she'd simply brushed the idea away, believing that her father—and his family—would want nothing to do with her.

"Look at Tamra's hair, Mom," Brady said with pride in his voice. "I'll never forget when your hair looked so much like that. Do you remember, Mom?"

Rayna's eyes said that she did. Following a lengthy silence while Tamra discreetly wiped at her tears, Brady motioned Jess forward and said to his mother, "This is Tamra's fiancé, Jess Hamilton. He's from Australia."

Jess took the old woman's hand and bent to look into her eyes. "It is such an honor to meet you," he said with perfect respect. "Brady tells me we have you to thank for Tamra having this beautiful red hair." He kissed her hand. "I'm counting on my own children getting some of it."

Following another silence, Brady said to Tamra, "Tell her what you've been doing. Tell her what you told me; show her the pictures. She understands everything you're saying."

Tamra nodded and did just that. While she talked, she was surprised when Brady pulled some nail clippers from his pocket to gently trim and file a snag on one of his mother's fingernails. He had obviously done it many times. Rayna's pleasure from the visit was evident, and Tamra couldn't suppress her disappointment when a nurse came to get her ready for bed. But Rayna was obviously tired, which kept Tamra from protesting. Before she was wheeled away, Tamra took her hand once more and said, "Thank you for a wonderful visit, Grandma. I'll come and see you again before I leave the country."

Once again, Rayna's eyes smiled. Jess spoke with her for a minute, and Brady and Claudia offered a comfortable good night. Then she was taken back to her room.

Once outside, Tamra quickly said to her father, "That was one of the greatest experiences of my life." Brady smiled in a way that fully expressed his pride and appreciation.

"She's an amazing woman," Brady said. "I'm sure your visit was equally meaningful to her."

"I hope so," Tamra said and they moved toward their parked vehicles.

"Are you in a hurry to get anywhere?" Brady asked, glancing at his watch. "We'd love to have you come over to the house. We're only a couple of minutes away, and tomorrow is Saturday so we don't need to get to bed early."

"Oh, that would be great," Claudia said. "And we've got some really good ice cream in the freezer."

Tamra turned to Jess, who checked her eyes before he said, "That sounds nice. We'll follow you."

Alone in the car with Jess, Tamra laughed out loud. "I can't believe it. That is just so neat."

Jess chuckled and took her hand. "Maybe your grandmother is the biggest reason you were prompted to come here."

"Maybe," she said, liking the idea. Her thoughts returned to the concerns she'd been feeling before they'd stopped at the care center. She knew it was important to ask her father about his absence in her life, and she prayed the opportunity would present itself without being too awkward. The sooner she got it out of the way, the more she could relax and enjoy what was turning out to be a rather nice day.

There wasn't time to think about it any further as Jess pulled into a long driveway behind her father. They all went together through the front door of a split-level brick home. A lamp that had been left burning in the front room illuminated tasteful, modest furnishings and surroundings that were fine without being ostentatious. Claudia immediately motioned to the pictures of her children and grandson on the wall, while she told them a little about each one. Brady took their coats and returned to invite them to sit down. Only then did Tamra notice two framed pictures on an end table near a lamp: one of her as a young child, and the other of her brother, Melvin.

She felt almost emotional to see them there; the frames were fine and beautiful, and their resting place was highly conspicuous. She hated the suspicious feeling that rose in her, making her wonder if they had been set out just today, since she might be coming by.

Claudia interrupted her thoughts, saying, "I'm going to dish up some ice cream. Does everybody want some?"

"I do," Jess said.

"It sounds great," Tamra added. "Can I help?"

"No, I'll help her," Brady said. "You just relax a minute."

Tamra reached over and picked up the picture of herself, and something trembled inside of her to see the dust marks left in its absence. It had been there much longer than today.

"Is that you?" Jess said, taking it from her.

"It is," she said and their eyes met. No words were necessary for her to know that he was well aware of what it meant to see this evidence that her father had been mindful of her all these years.

"Isn't that the cutest picture?" Brady said as he entered the room with two bowls of ice cream that he handed to Jess and Tamra. She set the picture aside and took a taste as Claudia entered with two bowls for herself and Brady.

"This is good," Jess said. "I don't think I've ever had this before."

"Oh, we like *unique* ice cream," Claudia said. "This has little peanut-butter cups in it."

"It's great," Tamra said.

They shared more comfortable small talk while they enjoyed dessert, then Claudia took the bowls to the kitchen and brought tall glasses of ice water to the front room and set them on coasters. Tamra took a sip of her water and set it back down, her eyes drawn back to the picture of herself. Given the present lack of conversation, it wasn't terribly difficult to say, "I have to admit, I was surprised to find a picture of myself here . . . like this."

Brady looked stunned, but not upset. "Why would you be?" he asked, almost as if the question had pained him.

Tamra took a deep breath and tried to gather the right words. Feeling Jess discreetly squeeze her hand, she felt sure he knew where she was headed. "It's just that . . ." She glanced down and smoothed a hand over her skirt, then she looked directly at her father. "I've spent my life without you. And . . . forgive me if it's inappropriate, but I just have to ask . . . Why? Why did I never have a father in my life?"

Tamra saw Claudia reach for Brady's hand, which was visibly trembling. Their eyes met and she sensed some level of anguish from him, but she didn't know him well enough to know if what she sensed was accurate. When the silence grew too long, she added, "Maybe you would prefer that I didn't ask such a question," she said. "Or perhaps—"

"No, Tamra, I'm glad you asked me . . . I've wanted very much to explain, but I just didn't know how to bring it up without sounding like a fool. It's just . . . not an easy question to answer. So please . . . be patient with me."

"I'm not in any hurry," Tamra said.

Claudia moved her hand to Brady's shoulder. Brady nervously rubbed his fingers together and gave a tense chuckle. "I . . . don't know where to start." He coughed and rubbed a hand over his face. His emotion was too evident to be phony—unless he was a *really* good actor. "To tell the truth, I've had this conversation in my head a thousand times . . . maybe more. I can't count the times I've wished that I could see you again . . . that I could just have the chance to tell my side of the story, and to let you know that in spite of how things turned out . . . I always loved you, always *wanted* to have you in my life."

Tamra squeezed Jess's hand, grateful beyond words to have him with her as she attempted to digest what she was hearing.

"I suppose," Brady went on, "the best place to start is at the beginning. The thing is . . ." He chuckled tensely. "This isn't easy to admit to your own daughter, but . . . the truth of the matter is that I married Myrna when she got pregnant. We'd been dating for a while, and I cared for her, in spite of being immature and ignorant. I was prepared to take responsibility for what I'd done. We did pretty good together at the start. After Mel was born, I realized she wasn't terribly fond of motherhood, but she did all right, and we traded work shifts so I could be with Mel when she couldn't. You came along soon after, and the two of you together were the best thing that ever happened to me. But it wasn't long before Myrna started staying out all night, and I knew she was drinking a lot more than she should. I did my best to just handle the situation and take care of you kids. I kept hoping we could work through it and she could go back to the way she used to be. Then one day I realized she was never going to change. She'd gotten so she hardly gave any attention to you kids at all—until I told her I was leaving and taking the kids with me. She went ballistic. And what followed was an absolute nightmare for me."

Tamra felt chilled by the unmasked anguish in her father's eyes. Jess put his arm around her shoulders, letting her know that he sensed the enormity of all she was feeling. Claudia took Brady's hand and they exchanged a tender glance that seemed to give him the courage to go on.

"There's no point in going over the details," Brady said. "It's in the past, and I've had to work very hard to leave it there. Let me put it this way—the custody battle got really ugly. I did my best to be honest, and to tell the judge exactly how I felt; I told him I loved my kids, and I knew I wasn't perfect, but I was working on my problems and I could be a good father. But Myrna, she . . ." There was a painful hesitation. "She produced witnesses that lied under oath, saying horrible things about me. And she told the judge exactly what he wanted to hear. I didn't even get visitation rights. By then, I was broke and in debt from all the court costs, and . . . I'm ashamed to say, that's when I started drinking too much. If I couldn't see my kids, I just didn't know how I could go on. After a while . . . I just kind of sank into a hole and gave up on everything."

Tamra felt an odd sense of relief from her father's explanation, but she couldn't deny the inkling of doubt that came with it. She didn't know her father well enough to know if he was telling the truth. Instinctively she believed he was. Or perhaps she just wanted so very badly to believe it was true. She sensed that he was waiting for some kind of response, but she felt her throat tightening with emotion, and was relieved when Brady went on to say, "I moved in with my mother when I left, and stayed with her through the divorce. She helped me through a great deal, but she made it clear that she wouldn't put up with the drinking and wallowing. I left for a long while; I don't remember how long. Those were dark years. I finally crawled back to her doorstep, barely alive, I believe. She took me in on the condition that I get a job and keep it, and help around the house. More than once she kicked me out and I wandered the streets for a while, but she always took me back. That last time, however, she told me she wouldn't put up with it anymore. And that's when I started going to those AA meetings." He sighed deeply. "I owe a great deal to my mother; if not for her courage to stand up to me—especially when I was being so difficult—I shudder to think where I would be."

Jess put his arm around Tamra and said, "Your daughter is a great deal like your mother in that respect."

"I'm not surprised," Brady said, interest sparkling in his eyes. But they darkened again and he turned to Tamra, as if to say there were other more important matters to address, and he would have to hear more about that later. He leaned forward and put his forearms on his thighs. He sighed and looked directly at her. "Now, I have a difficult question to ask *you*, Tamra . . . if that's all right."

Tamra nodded, unable to speak.

"I can't begin to tell you the endless hours I have worried over you and your brother. Knowing there were many things about your mother's lifestyle that I disagreed with, I've feared what you might be subjected to. It's obvious you've grown up to be a fine woman . . . in spite of your parents. But I need you to tell me . . . Were you all right? Did she take good care of you and your brother?"

Tamra felt momentarily stunned. Her view of her father misted over then cleared again as the tears spilled. Seeing his concerned eyes and furrowed brow, she quickly stammered, "I . . . can't talk about that . . . right now."

Feeling her emotion intensify, she leapt to her feet, logically assessing that a bathroom was down the hall to the left. But she'd barely taken a step when her father rose and gently took her arm. "Please, Tamra," he said gently, looking into her eyes, "I know it's hard . . . but I have to know."

Tamra squeezed her eyes shut and looked at the floor. "I'm . . . trying to put all of that behind me. I . . . I . . . just want to . . ." Her words became lost in a flood of tears.

Jess stood and put his hands on Tamra's shoulders. At the same moment, Brady met his eyes with a helpless pleading. Silently praying for guidance, Jess muttered behind her ear, "If you can't talk about it right now, that's okay. But I think you'll both be able to get past this a lot better in the long run if you talk it through." He lowered his voice to a whisper and added, "I'll hold your hand."

Tamra swallowed carefully and sniffled. She marveled at Jess's ability to march through the pain and confusion and pull her toward the light. She'd held his hand through many difficult moments in his own healing, and now he was here, carrying her through some of the most difficult moments of her life. She turned to meet his eyes, silently pleading for strength, and not surprised at how quickly she found it staring back at her. As if he could read her mind, he said quietly, "Just tell him and get it over with. Tell him the way you told me and be done with it."

Tamra coughed to avoid sobbing and admitted, "It was easier then."

"The best things in life are never easy," he said, reminding Tamra of his mother; Emily Hamilton was known for saying such things. And he was so much like her. She didn't know where he'd come up with so much strength in the weeks since his own life had seemed to be falling apart, but she felt unspeakably grateful to have him here for her now.

Tamra squeezed her eyes shut and prayed for the words to come to her mind, and for the courage to say them. The words that came were not what she'd expected, but they forced their way to her lips.

Her eyes remained closed, her voice faltered, but she managed to say, "There was a time when I fantasized constantly about you coming to rescue me. And one day I just stopped. I knew nobody was going to make it stop but me. So I did."

Jess saw Brady's face tighten, and the horror in his eyes was evident. With trembling fingers he lifted Tamra's chin and said gently, "Look at me, Tamra." She slowly opened her eyes and he added, "Make *what* stop?"

Tamra glanced toward Jess, who nodded firmly. She turned back to her father and just forced herself to say it. She felt surprisingly emotionless as the words spilled. "Nearly every man she brought home found a way to take advantage of me . . . in one way or another."

Brady's eyes narrowed and she could feel his trembling increase where he still held her chin. "Are you saying what I think you're saying?"

The words she'd once said to Jess came back to her, making her grateful for his advice as she was able to say, "If you can imagine the worst . . . that's what I'm saying. But don't try to imagine it. Don't even think about it; it's far too ugly. And it's in the past."

Brady's stunned expression melted with the sob that escaped his throat. He took Tamra into his arms and she could feel him shaking as he cried like a baby into her hair. Once Tamra comprehended that this man—practically a stranger, but her father nevertheless—could have so much regret and compassion on her behalf, she took hold of him as tightly as he held her. Through his tears she heard him say, "I should have rescued you, Tamra; I should have. I should have been man enough to take care of my own children." He pulled back and took her shoulders into his hands; tears streaked his face. "I don't know how you could ever forgive me for abandoning you that way."

Tamra took in her father's tormented expression while a volcano of emotion bubbled inside of her, threatening to erupt. Her only tangible thought was, "I . . . think I need to go . . . I'm tired and . . . I need to be alone for a while."

"Of course," Brady said, stepping back.

Tamra wanted to ease his obvious concern but she had to concentrate on holding back an emotional outburst.

"Will we see you again before you go?" he asked, as if he feared he'd *never* see her again.

Tamra nodded firmly, grateful for Jess's insight as he spoke for her. "Of course. Perhaps tomorrow we could . . ."

"Just call us in the morning," Claudia said. "We don't have any plans."

"We'll do that," Jess said, ushering Tamra toward the door. "And thank you . . . for everything."

Tamra hesitated at the door and met her father's eyes. While she was afraid to speak, she had no trouble hugging him briefly, and then Claudia. They both seemed relieved as Brady said, "It's been one of the best days of my life . . . in spite of the trauma. I'll look forward to seeing you tomorrow."

Tamra nodded again and Jess guided her to the car. The moment the door was closed, she broke into heaving sobs. She curled her arms around herself, barely managing to breathe.

"What can I do?" Jess asked.

"Just drive," she said and cried until her head pounded, while Jess kept his hand tightly in hers. She pulled a little package of tissues out of her purse and used one after another, tossing them on the floor.

"It's snowing again," Jess commented and said nothing more.

Her emotions had calmed to an occasional whimper by the time they reached the motel. Jess took her to her room and unlocked the door for her. "Do you want me to—"

"Please stay a while," she said. "I think I need to talk."

"I can agree with you there," he said and followed her into the room. But Tamra just sat in a chair and said nothing. Jess scooted the other chair to face her and sat down, leaning forward. "You're not saying much," he reported, as if she might not have noticed.

"I don't know what to say."

"Well," he drawled, "overall I'd say it was a pretty successful day. We spent time with your father and got to know him; we met your grandmother. And you asked your father what you needed to know. Apparently we cleared up some myths and—"

"Maybe that's the problem," Tamra interrupted. "It just . . . hit me like a brick that . . . well, I've been living with a lie. I always hated living with my mother. Instinctively I think I believed right from the start that it was all wrong . . . the abuse, her lack of love for me. And I guess it all just hit me again when he said what he did." She groaned and added, "I just can't believe it. It's like . . . spending your whole life believing that the earth is flat, and then suddenly finding out that it's round." She shook her head. "My mother lied to me. She told me he was a creep, and she fought to keep me away from him so I wouldn't discover the truth."

"The truth being that *he* left *her* because of her problems."

"That's right. And now . . . to think that all my life I've believed my father was a horrible person. He certainly had his problems, but . . . if I believe what my father told me, then—"

"*Do* you believe him?" Jess asked.

Tamra thought about it a minute. "Yes, I do. I must admit I had some moments of skepticism, but I've learned a lot in my life about being able to discern a lie—mostly because my mother is a great liar. I really think he's telling the truth, and I just . . . wish it could have been different."

"That's understandable," Jess said. "But you can't change the past, and regret won't help. So, as I see it, you're going to have to move forward from this moment and create a relationship with your father based on the present, not the past."

Tamra felt his words penetrate her clouded mind and she inhaled deeply. "My father," she whispered, as if the words were magical. She gave a wan smile. "You know, I really like him."

"So do I," Jess said and leaned back in his chair. A moment later he added, "So, you're all right with seeing them again tomorrow?"

"Of course," she said.

"Well . . . I have a hunch there's something he's going to want to know . . . that he *needs* to know. And whether or not he asks, I think you need to be prepared to tell him."

"What?" she asked, her heart quickening. The thought of another heart-wrenching conversation with her father held no appeal.

Jess took a deep breath and leaned forward again. "Have you forgiven him, Tamra?" When she didn't answer he went on. "You understand now that his absence in your life was not of his own choosing, but he still had a drinking problem that contributed to his not being able to make a difference for you. I don't think anyone would blame you for feeling some anger toward him . . . considering everything that happened to you that he could have prevented had the situation been different."

Tamra thought about it for a minute. "But it's in the past. He's changed; he's put it behind him. He's a good man. And he's obviously very sorry."

"Yes, I agree."

"So . . . of course I've forgiven him," she said.

"Do you really feel that, Tamra? Or are you just saying it because it's the right thing to say?" She looked confused, so he added, "As I understand it, the Lord has commanded us to forgive others, but that doesn't mean it happens with the snap of your fingers just because you want it to. Sometimes we have some feelings to work through first. And it's better to work through them than to claim forgiveness before you feel it."

Tamra took his hand and squeezed it. "Your mother taught you that, didn't she?"

Jess smiled. "How did you know?"

"It just sounds like something she would say."

"Well, yes she did. And I've yet to hear my mother give bad advice. She is a very wise woman."

"Yes, she is. And I want to think about what you said . . . and pray about it."

"I think that's a good idea." Jess came to his feet. "So, I'm going to my room and we're both going to get some sleep, and we'll talk again in the morning."

"Thank you," she said, squeezing his hand.

"For what?" he asked.

"A thousand things . . . but mostly just for loving me, and helping me get through this."

"A pleasure, darlin'," he said, much like his father would to his mother. Then he kissed her good night.

Following a good, long prayer, Tamra crawled into bed and gazed at the ceiling above her. Now that she'd gotten past the trauma of a difficult—but necessary—conversation with her father, she felt incredibly grateful for the events of this day. The idea of having a father and grandmother in her life seemed magical and surreal. But it *was* real. And she could hardly sleep as she replayed the changes that had occurred in her life in a matter of hours. She forced herself to relax, anticipating the opportunity to spend time with them again tomorrow.

In spite of not falling asleep until around two, Tamra woke early and took a quick shower. She was barely dressed when she called Jess's room and he groggily answered the phone. "Get out of bed, Hamilton," she said. "I want to see my family." She laughed at the feel of such words coming through her own lips.

"Yes, ma'am," he said and chuckled.

Twenty minutes later he knocked at her door and she was ready to go. "Do you think it's too early to call them?" she asked once he'd kissed her in greeting.

They both glanced at the clock on the bedside table. Eight thirty-three. "Go for it," he said and she hurried toward the phone.

It only rang once before she heard her father's voice eagerly say, "Hello?"

"Hi, Dad," she said.

"Tamra?" he asked in a voice that almost moved her to tears. She had to wonder if he'd somehow believed that she wouldn't call or come back, and they'd never see each other again.

"Did I wake you?" she asked, forcing her voice to sound normal.

"No, no. I'm glad you called. I was just going to cook breakfast. Have you eaten?"

"No, but you don't have to—"

"I don't want to be pushy," he said, "but we'd love to have you. What do you say?"

"Okay," Tamra said. "We'll be there soon. Is there something we can bring?"

"Just yourselves," Brady said and Tamra laughed as soon as she hung up the phone.

"What?" Jess asked.

"We're invited to breakfast."

"Cool," Jess said and motioned toward the door. In the car, he said, "So, did you think about it?"

"Yes," she said, needing no explanation.

"And?" he drawled expectantly. She just let out a little laugh and looked out the window.

Brady and Claudia both met them at the door, obviously pleased to see them. Wanting to clear the air from last night, Tamra was relieved when her father took her shoulders into his hands and immediately said, "Are you feeling better this morning? I didn't mean to upset you, but—"

"I'm fine," she said, "and just so you don't have to wonder . . . I want you to know that I *have* forgiven you. I must admit there have been many times in my life that I've felt angry toward you, but I learned a long time ago that it's not my place to judge, and it's not up to me to carry the burden of other people's choices, even when they've hurt me." She felt a desire to explain her testimony of the Atonement, but felt certain now was not the right time. Keeping to the point, she pressed forward. "Now that I understand the situation from your point of view, it's made a big difference for me. It's in the past, and I think we should start over from this day to be as a father and daughter should be."

Moisture rose into Brady's eyes before Tamra hugged him tightly, feeling him return it with a fervor that filled a hole inside her that she had believed would forever be empty.

Jess and Tamra went with Brady and Claudia into the kitchen, where bacon was frying and the waffle iron was heating. They worked together to put breakfast on, talking and laughing as if they'd all known each other for years. When they sat down to eat and it became evident that saying a prayer over the food was not customary in the home, Tamra ventured to say, "Do you mind if we bless it? Only if you're comfortable with it, of course."

Brady looked surprised but didn't seem concerned. "That would be fine," he said. Claudia smiled and Tamra uttered a brief prayer, including her gratitude for being reunited with loved ones. After the amen had been spoken, Tamra looked up to see Brady reaching for Claudia's hand across the corner of the table. He smiled at Tamra and they began to eat, continuing their conversation long after the meal was finished. They shared experiences from their lives, and speculations over things they would do together in the future. Brady told them more about his mother's health problems, and it was obvious that Rayna had been living with them when she'd had her stroke. Claudia spoke of her mother-in-law with love and respect, and it was evident she had put many hours into caring for her. Tamra felt comforted in a way that was difficult to define. Just to know that she had family connections with good, decent people touched her deeply.

While Brady and Jess loaded the dishwasher, Tamra helped Claudia clear the table and wash the pans. When they were finished, Brady took Jess to show him something or other in the garage, while Claudia and Tamra sat down in the family room just off the dining area.

"While we have a minute alone," Claudia said, reaching for Tamra's hand, "I just want to tell you that . . . your coming here, and what you said this morning . . . you will never know what that means to your father. He's had so much anguish over losing you and wondering about you. Of course, he knows where your brother is, and he's tried to see him. But with you . . . he just didn't know, and it's eaten at him. I think he suspected there were awful things going on in your home when you were children, and it's haunted him. As difficult as it was last night, I'm glad you told him. Now he doesn't have to wonder. But you should know . . ." Claudia's eyes filled with tears, but she smiled brightly through them. "Last night after you left, he said at least half a dozen times, 'I'd give anything if she could just forgive me, but I don't know how she ever could.' When you walked in and said what you did, it just . . ." Her voice cracked and Tamra impulsively hugged her. "You will never know what peace you have given him, Tamra my dear."

Tamra felt too emotional to speak, but she nodded in firm agreement as she drew back and squeezed her stepmother's hand. She felt profoundly grateful for gospel principles that had helped her understand that forgiving her father and letting go of the past was the only possible way to move forward. She was also grateful for the warmth of the Spirit that had prompted her to accept the Savior's invitation to shift the burden to His shoulders. Considering the changes her father had made in his life, she swallowed her emotions and finally managed to say to Claudia, "I'm glad he has you."

"I'm glad I have him," Claudia said. "He's a good man, Tamra. His father died when he was very young, and I think that was one of the biggest reasons he became such a rebellious youth. But I believe most of us have to face some hard knocks in this life. It's what we do with them that makes us who we are."

Tamra nodded in agreement and the men entered the room. "Hey," Brady said, "it's too bad you're headed back to Australia. I was thinking of all the holidays we haven't been able to share. It sure would be great to share Christmas."

While Tamra was trying to think of an appropriate response, Claudia said brightly, "I remember when I was a kid, and my uncle was in the Marines. He got leave in October, and the family had Christmas while he was there. They put up the tree and exchanged gifts and had a big dinner. It was great! Why don't we do that? We could pull it together in a couple of days, and we'll take lots of pictures and make some great memories while you're here." She laughed and added, "I mean . . . I always put everything up before Thanksgiving anyway; I'd only be a couple of weeks ahead—give or take a little."

Tamra glanced at Jess, who said eagerly, "I don't see why not. I think it sounds fantastic."

"Great," Brady said and the others laughed.

"So, when should we have this Christmas celebration?" Claudia asked. Then more to her husband, "Is your work tight at the first of the week?"

"Actually no," he said. "Since I got that inspection over with yesterday, I think they can do without me for a couple of days."

"Great," Claudia said and laughed again. "So . . . Monday or Tuesday? What works best for you?" she asked Jess and Tamra.

"We're not in any hurry," Tamra said. "You should say what's best for you. We don't want you going to a lot of trouble or—"

"Oh, it's no trouble. We'll just stick to the basics. Let's plan on Monday being Christmas Eve—figuratively speaking, of course. And Tuesday will be our Christmas day. Does that sound all right?"

"It sounds wonderful," Tamra said, and couldn't hold back a burst of laughter.

Chapter Five

They all went together to the care center to see Rayna. This time they found her in her own room, which was filled with evidence of Brady and Claudia's love for her. There were many cards taped to the closet door, fresh flowers, and a conglomeration of little gifts they had obviously given to her. As Tamra asked questions about certain pictures and little trinkets sitting about, Claudia and Brady explained in a way that kept Rayna's attention. Claudia's children and grandchild were apparently common visitors to Rayna, as well. Tamra learned then that she also had an aunt and an uncle. Rayna had two other children who both lived out of state and had little to do with their mother.

Tamra whispered to Jess, "It would seem that my father is the cream of the crop."

"As are you," Jess said, surprising her. But as she sat to visit with her grandmother, tightly holding her hand, she had to admit it felt great to think that she had inherited something innately good in her character from this woman, through her father, who had eventually come to find the good in himself. Their visit was not as long as Tamra would have liked, since Rayna obviously tired quickly. Tamra loved being with her grandmother, in spite of their one-sided conversations.

They returned to the house and discussed their early Christmas celebration. With plans made for the next few days, Tamra told her father and Claudia that they had some things to do and would see them tomorrow.

"Will you come early?" Claudia asked expectantly.

"Actually," Tamra said, "we'll be going to church in the morning. We should be out by early afternoon." She figured they could find a nine o'clock meeting somewhere that would be out by noon.

"Can you make it for lunch, then?" Claudia asked. "And then we could trim the tree and maybe do a little baking."

"It sounds great," Tamra said, then turned to Jess. "Is that all right with you, Mr. Hamilton?"

"It's perfect," he said and they all shared embraces at the door.

In the car, Jess asked, "So what is it that we have to do?"

"What?" Tamra asked, momentarily disoriented.

"You said we had some things to do. I'm just wondering what it is . . . or did you need a little space?"

"Some of both, perhaps," she admitted. "But if you must know, there's a great deal that we have to do."

"Such as?" he asked, backing the car out of the driveway.

"Christmas shopping, of course," she said and Jess laughed.

"Of course."

"Also," Tamra said after they'd driven in silence for a few minutes, "it occurred to me this morning that I should visit the family that supported me on my mission."

"I'd love to meet them," Jess said, obviously pleased.

"So, let's go back to the motel. I'll try to call them, change my shoes, and we'll go shopping."

Jess laughed again. "Sounds delightful." He reached for her hand and brought it to his lips. "But then . . . life has become a whole lot more delightful since you came into it."

"The feeling is mutual," she said and kissed his cheek.

Tamra phoned the Wallace family and was pleased when Sister Wallace answered the phone. She was thrilled to hear from Tamra and said they'd be delighted to see her and meet her fiancé. They would be going out on some errands this afternoon, but would be home in the evening.

"Why don't you come for supper?" Sister Wallace asked.

"Oh, you don't need to—"

"We'd love to have you," she interrupted Tamra. "Unless you have plans, of course."

"Well, that would be fine; just don't go to any trouble."

"You're practically family," Sister Wallace said. "How much trouble can you be? We'll see you around seven."

"We'll be there," Tamra said and hung up the phone.

"Okay," she said to Jess, "dinner at the Wallaces' at seven. Let's get shopping."

Tamra guided Jess to what she told him was the world's largest mall. "The Mall of America," she said dramatically. "And there's an amusement park inside."

"Really?" he said dubiously.

"Really," she repeated. "But you have to see it to believe it."

"Well," he said, parking the car, "if we can't find something here, we're out of luck." He chuckled and added, "If nothing else, we can get some good exercise walking through it."

Going inside, Jess asked, "Have you got anything in mind?"

"Not particularly," she said. "What do you buy for people you love but you don't know?"

"That's a good question. We'll just . . . try to be inspired."

After looking for more than two hours with no success, Jess declared, "Maybe a ride on that roller coaster will unclog our brains."

They rode on the roller coaster, and a log flume as well, making Tamra feel that she really was on vacation. When that was done, Jess said, "That was certainly fun, and we've had a great tour of the mall, but I think we'd better take a lunch break. I'm starving."

Over lunch, Tamra picked at her food and prayed silently for some guidance in finding the right gifts for her father, stepmother, and grandmother. Jess interrupted her prayer, saying, "I think you need gifts that will share with them something that's meaningful to you."

"Like what?" she asked.

"Well, what means a lot to you? What's important in your life?"

"The gospel . . . but I don't want to be pushy with that. I just don't feel like it's the right time. My example over time will mean more."

"I agree," he said. "So, what else?"

"Australia," she said with a little smile.

"So, we'll get them a koala bear," he said, obviously not serious.

"I get the feeling you're fishing for something here, Jess. Why don't you just tell me what's on your mind?"

"Okay, I will," he said. "When I think of things that are meaningful to you . . . things that make you unique, one of the first things that comes to mind is the way you diligently keep a journal, and your love for genealogy." Tamra's heart quickened as he went on. "I'll never forget when I found you in the library, snooping around for my family history records."

Tamra looked into his eyes and felt the memories wash over her. "I remember how you sat beside me on the floor . . . touching my hair as if you had a right to. And we were practically strangers."

"Yes we were," he said. "But it didn't feel like it then any more then than it does now. It feels like we've known each other forever."

Tamra felt a chill rush up her back, as if to confirm the truth of his words. The intensity of his expression let her know he was feeling the same way, even before he reached over the table to kiss her, whispering close to her lips, "I love you, Tamra Banks. You're the best thing that ever happened to me."

Tamra sighed and touched his face. "The feeling is mutual, Jess."

He kissed her again and leaned back in his chair. "So," he said, as if they hadn't just shared a deep spiritual connection, sitting in the middle of a crowded mall, "I think you should get your father and stepmother each a nice journal, and perhaps some stationery to encourage letter writing. E-mail is nice, but I know you. You like old-fashioned letters on paper."

Tamra smiled. "Yes, you're right. And I think that's a wonderful idea. Hurry and eat. I know just where to go."

"Okay, but we have plenty of time. Finish your lunch."

Tamra fought back her excitement and forced herself to eat. She was pleased to find some beautiful leather-bound journals that she purchased for her father and stepmother, along with some fine pens that weren't terribly expensive. She didn't know if they had ever kept journals, or if they ever would, but she figured it was still a nice gift and it might inspire them to record something of their lives.

Tamra bought a lead crystal hanging from fine thread, cut into the shape of a heart. It was meant to hang in a window so that the sunlight would shine through it and cast sparkling light around the room. She felt it was the ideal gift for her grandmother.

Tamra liked Jess's idea of stationery, and found some lovely boxed sets. They purchased gift wrap, bows, scissors, tape, and some personal Christmas cards. For the first time in her life, she was grateful for the commercialism of Christmas that made such things available early in November. Walking out of the mall, she still felt like she should get them something else. Silently she debated the obvious possibilities: a box of chocolates, a keepsake Christmas ornament, something to wear. She didn't want to overdo it, but then this was meant to make up for many lost Christmases, and it might be a long time before she returned to the States to see them again.

Tamra stopped walking as an idea occurred to her. Jess took a few steps then turned around. "What?"

"I know what else to get them," she announced.

"Okay," he said. He nodded with exaggerated expectation when she said nothing.

"You said it over lunch." She laughed softly. "But it just kicked in, I suppose."

"What?"

"Genealogy," she said. "I have my laptop and all my disks. We can find a copy center, print off the records, and put them in a binder." She smiled. "And I can do a copy for my grandmother."

Jess grinned. "No gift could mean more, in my opinion." He glanced at his watch. "However, it will have to wait until Monday. We've got a dinner appointment."

Tamra gasped. "I almost forgot."

They hurried to the car and put their purchases into the trunk. Tamra gave Jess directions to the Wallaces' home while she told him how she had come to know them. When Sister Wallace had been assigned to be her visiting teacher, Tamra had been living in an apartment with a roommate at the time, but was still working with her mother and brother. Sister Wallace had tuned in quickly to the challenges in Tamra's life, and began inviting Tamra to be involved with their family of five children, ranging at the time from kindergarten to a son serving a mission. They had encouraged Tamra to serve a mission, and had eagerly offered to support her. Their family furniture business was thriving and they were glad to use their prosperity to help her. Tamra had kept in touch with them through letters during and since her mission, but she couldn't leave Minneapolis without seeing them.

Brother Wallace answered the door and laughed as he enveloped Tamra in a bear hug. She had always thought he looked like Santa Claus—minus the beard. And he had a jolly laugh to enhance his appearance.

Tamra hugged him back, then motioned to Jess. "Brother Wallace, this is my fiancé, Jess Hamilton."

"Brother Hamilton," he said, eagerly shaking Jess's hand. "Come in. Come in. It's cold out there." He called as he closed the door, "Amelia, dear. They're here."

Amelia rushed into the room, as plump and bright as her husband, smoothing a hand through her graying hair that hung straight to the top of her shoulder. "Oh, my goodness." She laughed and hugged Tamra. "You've not changed a bit, my dear." She turned to Jess. "And this must be the lucky man."

"I am indeed," Jess said.

"You're not American," Brother Wallace said, as if the fact were delightful and intriguing.

"My mother is American," Jess said proudly. "And my father Australian."

"Which is where you have obviously spent most of your life," Brother Wallace said, motioning them to the sofa in the front room.

"Yes," Jess said, "although I have spent some years off and on in the States."

The conversation moved smoothly along, eventually carrying them to the dinner table where Amelia served a casserole, a Jell-O salad, red punch, fresh vegetables, and chocolate cake. The two younger children were the only ones at home, since one was now married, another on a mission, and another out on a date. Tamra marveled at how they had all grown, and after dinner was cleaned up, they took turns looking at photographs that helped fill in the years. The Wallaces encouraged mission stories from Tamra, insisting that they had earned a report they'd never fully gotten since she had gone straight from her mission to Australia. She enjoyed recounting experiences she'd not even thought about for a while, and they liked the story of how she had met Jess's parents while serving in the Philippines.

When they realized it was getting late, Tamra was grateful for an invitation to attend church with the Wallaces tomorrow. Their meetings began at nine, which would get them through in time to get to her father's, but they would have the opportunity to see the Wallaces again in the morning.

On the way back to the motel, Jess said, "That was nice. They're a wonderful family."

"Yes, they are."

"And it's apparent they adore you," he said. "But then, who wouldn't?" He kissed her hand and laughed softly. Tamra just smiled.

Tamra thoroughly enjoyed church the following day. She saw many people she had once known while living in this ward. And it was a pleasure to introduce them to Jess. It was hard to say good-bye to the Wallaces following the meetings, but they promised to keep in touch.

After changing clothes at the motel, they drove to Brady and Claudia's home. Claudia answered the door, wearing jeans and a festive Christmas sweatshirt. Stepping into the house, Tamra immediately felt the transformation since they had been there the previous morning. The house smelled of pine and spices; jarred candles on the coffee table were obviously responsible for adding such sweet aromas to the atmosphere. *Fresh Aire* Christmas music was playing softly from a stereo in the corner of the front room. A beautiful, artificial Christmas tree had been assembled in the opposite corner, with a number of decorations and lights spread around the room, waiting to be put on the tree.

Claudia led them into the kitchen, where Brady was just pulling a pan out of the oven. He too was wearing a Christmas sweatshirt.

"Hello there," he said brightly, setting the pan on the stove.

They chatted comfortably while Brady sliced the roast beef, and Claudia made gravy at the stove. Tamra and Jess set the table after Brady showed them where to find everything they needed.

After they had eaten dinner and cleaned up, they settled into decorating the tree according to Claudia's directions. First the strings of tiny colored lights were plugged in and tested, then they were carefully wound into the branches while Christmas memories were exchanged. Tamra had to admit that she'd had a few good Christmases in her childhood, depending on who her mother happened to be married to at the time. She'd spent two good Christmases with families in her ward prior to her mission, one of those families being the Wallaces. The one Christmas she'd spent in the Philippines had been memorable but difficult, and the holidays she'd spent with her Aunt Rhea in Australia had been good. But never had she felt the spark that was coming to life inside her now. She could almost tangibly feel the love of her father and stepmother—for each other, and for her. And each time Jess met her eyes, she was reminded of how very blessed she was.

As the garland and dozens of little decorations slowly went onto the tree, Tamra forced her mind away from the heartache of all she'd missed out on through her troubled youth. Concentrating on the moment, she had to admit that she'd never enjoyed decorating a tree so much. The last thing to go on the tree was a silver star filled with tiny white lights. Brady stood on the stepladder to attach it to the top of the tree, then he plugged it into the light cord and it lit up brilliantly. They all applauded then sat to rest and admire their work. Tamra found herself mesmerized by the light flowing from the star, as if it somehow represented all the good things that had come into her life in the years since she had embraced the gospel.

Claudia picked up on her reflective mood and commented, "I searched long and hard for the perfect star. And I really love that one. I hope it never needs to be replaced."

"It *is* beautiful," Tamra said. "And a star is such a wonderful symbol, don't you think? It's something that gives light and guides you through the darkness. I guess that's one of many reasons it's the perfect thing to put on top of a Christmas tree."

"So it is," Claudia said, gazing up at the star again.

Tamra felt an urge to take her analogy a step further, of how the star that guided the wise men to Jesus symbolized how we should all follow the example of the Savior, who was the Light of the World. But she had no idea of their feelings about Christianity, and she wanted to become a little more comfortable in their relationship before she expressed her opinions too freely.

They finally got up to gather the decoration boxes and put them away in the basement. Claudia then directed everyone into the kitchen, where three different projects were put into motion. They rolled out and baked little sugar cookies in Christmas shapes. And Claudia taught Tamra how to make a braided sweet bread with cherry pie filling in the center, which was baked in the shape of a candy cane. They carefully watched over the homemade fudge, and when it was left to set up they all sat down to frost and decorate little cookies, talking and laughing and making a mess like a bunch of kids.

Jess and Tamra left after ten o'clock with a plate of goodies to take back to the motel. They promised to return by four the following day to begin their Christmas Eve celebration, and Tamra couldn't deny a childlike excitement inside of her. She had trouble falling asleep that night as she pondered the events of the last few days, focusing only on the positive—of which there was plenty. She finally slept, anticipating the following day, and woke about nine. She called Jess's room to tell him she'd be ready in half an hour. He greeted her at the door with a kiss and she had to wonder what she'd ever done to deserve having such a good man in her life.

Following a quick breakfast, they found a full-service copy center where Tamra was able to print out copies of her genealogical records and have them bound. They ran into a few glitches, but they were solved quickly with the help of friendly employees. Glancing over the records with new interest, Tamra pointed out to Jess the name Geraldine R. Banks.

"Who is that?" Jess asked.

"My grandmother," she said. "That's why the name Rayna didn't sound familiar to me. It must be her middle name."

Over lunch, Jess said, "So, we go to the room and wrap these gifts, and we're ready for the big celebration, right?"

"I suppose," Tamra said.

"You don't sound convinced."

"Well . . . I just feel like I want to get them something else. I know that technically the gifts we have for them are sufficient, but . . . I have a feeling they're going to spoil us, and . . . even if they don't, well . . . the point is not trying to get even, but . . ."

"No, it's not. But if you feel like you want to get something else, we will. Do you have any ideas?"

"No." She sighed.

"I do," Jess said and she smiled.

"Are you telling me you had the same feeling?"

"Yes, actually," he said. "I was thinking . . . they have a lot of beautiful Christmas decor, and I'm assuming that perhaps not all of it has been put out, since we went about this rather quickly, but . . . I didn't see any kind of a nativity. I realize religion has not been a part of their lives, but maybe we could give them a nativity set. It's a suitable

Christmas gift, and a way for you to appropriately share some degree of your beliefs with them . . . without saying a word."

"I think it's a splendid idea," Tamra said. "And I remember seeing some in that store in the mall."

He laughed. *"That store* in the mall? I hope you can narrow it down a little better than that. Considering *that* mall, it could take a while."

"I know just where it is," she said and they hurried to the car.

They quickly found the right store, but it took Tamra nearly half an hour to decide which nativity set she wanted. There were several that captured the spirit and beauty of what they portrayed, but she wanted the one she chose to be perfect for her father and Claudia. She finally settled on a set of porcelain figures, handpainted in subdued colors. The stable was made from barn wood, with a white porcelain star attached to the front that stood out in brilliant contrast to the dark colors of the rest of the set.

The clerk wrapped each piece of the set separately in white tissue paper and put it into its original box; then she wrapped the box in red foil paper and tied a big silver ribbon around it. Tamra's excitement deepened as they returned to the motel and wrapped the other gifts before they headed for Brady and Claudia's home, arriving right on time. The Christmas music and aromas of the previous day struck Tamra's senses as she entered. But today, with the tree decorated, and its lights shining brightly, an intangible magic hovered in the air.

After their gifts were deposited beneath the tree, Jess and Tamra quickly became caught up in helping with some dinner preparations, while Claudia finished making a batch of divinity. She spooned the candy out onto waxed paper to set up, like neat little rows of fluffy white clouds.

When Brady got out the dishes and Tamra began helping him set the table, she noticed by the number of plates that more people were expected. As if he had read her mind, Brady said, "We invited the kids to join us for dinner. We thought it would be nice for you to get to know each other."

"Sounds wonderful," Tamra said, and folded the napkins into little triangles.

"And it's even Monday," Jess said. "It's like family home evening."

"What's that?" Claudia asked, intrigued.

"Well," Jess explained, "it's something our Church has established. Church members are encouraged to set aside one evening a week to be with our families. By setting Mondays aside, all other Church activities are scheduled for other nights, so there's no conflict."

"What a marvelous idea," Claudia said.

"Yeah," Jess said and winked at Tamra.

The magical feeling in the air increased as Claudia's children arrived with their spouses. And little one-year-old Jordan became the center of attention. Tamra thought of Evelyn and suddenly missed her deeply. Jess's three-year-old niece was often on Tamra's mind, but being around a toddler was a poignant reminder of the childish antics that had become so familiar to Tamra as she helped care for Evelyn.

Tamra loved the feel of belonging to a family as they talked and laughed and got to know each other over a classic holiday meal of roast turkey and all the trimmings. Later, after the dishes were done, Claudia set out the Christmas goodies they'd been making so the family could enjoy them while they played Pictionary and Guesstures.

The party finally broke up around ten, and everyone seemed to leave at once. With the house suddenly quiet except for the Christmas music that had never stopped playing throughout the evening, Brady said, "Well, you kids had better go back to your rooms and get some sleep. I made special arrangements for Santa Claus to come, and he won't be happy if he gets here and finds us still yakking the night away."

Tamra laughed and hugged her father. "Then I guess we'd better go."

"I can certainly take a hint," Jess said with mock indignation, and they all laughed.

In the car, Tamra said to Jess, "Wasn't that wonderful?"

"Yes, it was." He smiled and took her hand. "It would seem you've got a pretty decent family, after all."

"Some of them," Tamra said sadly and turned toward the window, hating the way thoughts of her mother put such a damper on her feelings, like a draft of cold air in an otherwise warm and cozy room. The effects of her mother's neglect and belligerence rippled through every aspect of her life, and she wondered if she could ever be free of such negative feelings.

At the motel, Jess opened Tamra's door before he pulled her into his arms and kissed her. She became briefly distracted from everything beyond her feelings for Jess. Even the cold air became nonexistent when she drew back and looked into his eyes.

"I love you, Tamra Banks," he muttered close to her face.

"And I love you," she replied, kissing him again.

"Merry Christmas," he added and smiled.

"Merry Christmas," she said, and he left her alone.

Tamra quickly got ready for bed and crawled between the covers, feeling the excitement of a child. She briefly thought of her mother and brother and wondered what they were doing, then she convinced herself that she didn't want to know. Instead, she concentrated on the fun she'd had this evening, and her anticipation of how wonderful tomorrow would be. And with that she slept.

A phone ringing broke into Tamra's sleep. She groped for it and heard Jess say like a child, "Do you think Santa came?"

"I don't know. What time is it?"

"Time we woke your parents and reminded them of how pesky children can be on Christmas morning. Besides, the sun is up . . . almost, and it's snowing."

"Really?" she asked, coherent now.

"Really." Jess laughed. "I'll be over to get you in ten minutes."

Tamra hung up the phone and rushed to the window. Pulling back the heavy drapes she let out a delighted gasp to see a beautiful snow falling amidst a predawn glow. She hurried to get dressed and they drove carefully to her father's home; she hoped they would be out of bed, in spite of Jess's desire to be *pesky*.

Claudia answered the door, wide awake with her makeup on, but wearing satiny pajamas that barely showed beneath a matching robe. "Good morning," she said brightly, and Tamra thought, as she often did, that the woman's smile could light up the darkest of days. "Isn't it a *beautiful* morning!" she added with fervor.

"It is indeed," Jess said. "Is Brady still in bed?"

"No, he'll be out in a minute."

"Too bad," Jess said. "I was hoping to go pounce on him and wake him up."

"I heard that," Brady said, appearing from the hallway. "Perhaps another time."

"Perhaps," Jess said and laughed.

Their attention turned to the corner of the front room where the tree lights shone brilliantly and a number of beautifully wrapped packages had been laid out around the tree.

"Oh, let's get started," Claudia said, betraying that she shared Tamra's excitement.

Brady insisted that Tamra open the first gift, a cream-colored silk sweater. "You have good taste," Tamra said to Claudia, holding it against herself. "I love it."

"Your father picked it out," Claudia said. "I just got the size right."

"Thank you," Tamra said, standing to quickly give them each a kiss on the cheek. "It's beautiful."

Jess opened the next gift, which was a navy-colored, long-sleeved polo shirt, much like the style he often wore. He was obviously pleased and Tamra declared, "He looks good in blue. If he wears blue, his eyes look blue, and if he wears green, they look green."

"And what if I wore orange?" Jess asked.

"You would look sick," Tamra said, and they all laughed. "I'm not terribly fond of orange."

"And when I wear white?" Jess asked.

"Your eyes are bluish-green."

"Of course," he said and handed gifts to Brady and Claudia.

They loved the journals, and while they both admitted they'd never kept personal journals, they seemed pleased with the idea of starting such a habit, especially when Tamra said, "I want my children and grandchildren to know you and what you were like."

Jess and Tamra then opened matching Minnesota sweatshirts, a gift certificate for dinner at a fine restaurant, and tickets to a symphony performance the following evening. "So you can have a nice date before you leave town," Brady said.

In turn, Brady and Claudia opened the pens and the stationery, obviously pleased with both. "You're really determined to have us do some writing, aren't you," Brady said.

"Yes, I am," Tamra said. "It doesn't have to be quantity, but . . . I love handwritten letters, and I was hoping we could start exchanging them."

"I'm looking forward to it," Brady said with a warm smile that penetrated Tamra's heart.

Tamra was touched when she opened a necklace with a delicate silver star hanging on a fine chain. Claudia explained, "When I saw it, I thought of what you'd said about the star on the Christmas tree. So the necklace is to remind you that no matter how far apart we are, you have family who loves you, and we'll always be here to help get you through whatever life might dish out."

Tamra became too emotional to speak but she rose to embrace Claudia, then her father, noting that they too had tears in their eyes. She sat back down and wiped the moisture from her face, silently thanking God for guiding her to her family.

Jess then opened a tiepin that was a masculine version of the silver star on Tamra's necklace. "And that's to remind you that you're part of the family as well," Brady said to him.

Jess promptly pinned it on his shirt collar and thanked them profusely. He then handed Claudia the package that contained the nativity, and Brady the wrapped genealogy book.

"You go first," Tamra said to Claudia. "These gifts are both for the two of you to share."

Claudia looked confused when she first opened the box, since it was filled with pieces wrapped in tissue paper, with only one edge of the wood stable showing. She took out one piece and unwrapped the figure of Mary, then she let out a delighted laugh.

"What is it?" Brady asked and Claudia laughed again, quickly unwrapping the next piece, which was a shepherd.

"It's a nativity set," she said, so genuinely pleased that Tamra couldn't suppress a silent surge of joy. Jess squeezed her hand and tossed her a gratified smile.

"We didn't know if you had one," Tamra said, "but—"

"We don't, actually," Claudia said. "I did at one time, but the pieces broke when the kids were little and I never replaced it. I've thought about getting one occasionally, but it just didn't happen." She opened the wise men, another shepherd, the animals, and finally the baby Jesus.

"Oh, it's so beautiful," she said, immediately setting the pieces up, along with the little stable, right next to the Christmas tree.

"And look at the star," Brady said, touching it where it shone brightly against the dark wood of the stable. "It's beautiful. Thank you, both of you."

"You're welcome," Jess and Tamra said together.

"We'll treasure it always," Claudia said.

Brady then opened the package he was holding. He too looked confused until Tamra said, "Those are copies of all the genealogical research I have done for your ancestors, both your mother's line and your father's line. I could only get one line back to the early sixteenth century, but the other one goes back to the mid-fourteen-hundreds."

Brady glanced up at Tamra, his expression incredulous. "This is astounding," he muttered and turned back to the book in his hands, flipping slowly through the pages.

Claudia scooted closer to him to look over his arm. For several minutes nothing was said, as they both seemed enthralled with the book. Claudia finally pointed to something and asked, "What does this mean?"

Tamra rose long enough to see Claudia pointing at the notations to indicate the temple work that had been completed. She sat back down and simply said, "In our Church, we believe that every person must have certain ordinances performed in order to return to live with our Father in Heaven. For those who have died without those opportunities, the work is performed in our temples by proxy. These notations indicate that these ordinances have been done for every person whose records I was able to find. They are now all sealed together as a family, eternally."

Brady and Claudia both glanced up at Tamra in the same moment, silently questioning what she meant. She quickly added, "We believe that when we are married in the temple, with the proper authority, that marriage and families don't end with death." Tamra reached for Jess's hand and added, "When we're married, it will be for time and all eternity—not until death do us part."

"And you really believe that?" Claudia asked, with more interest than skepticism.

"I do," Tamra said with conviction.

Brady and Claudia both turned their attention back to the book as Brady said, "Thank you, Tamra. I never even thought about having such records, but . . . it's truly wonderful."

"I'm glad you like it," Tamra said, squeezing Jess's hand again.

When the wrappings were all cleaned up, they worked together to prepare a late breakfast of waffles, sausage, and fresh fruit. The smell of coffee that Brady and Claudia were drinking reminded Tamra more of her time living with her aunt in Sydney than it did of her childhood, and she found the association somehow comforting.

After breakfast they all went together to visit Rayna at the care center. The snow had stopped and the clouds had cleared, creating a perfect Christmas day—even if they were just pretending. Rayna showed a vague expression of surprise when Tamra said they had an early Christmas gift for her. Jess helped her open the gift, and she was obviously pleased with the crystal heart. Brady hung it in her window where it glistened brightly, and Tamra explained to her that in the morning the sun would shine through it and make her whole room sparkle.

Brady opened the genealogy book and showed it to her, explaining in quite a bit of detail. He pointed out her own name on a pedigree chart and how it spread out to her ancestors. Again, her expressive eyes were obviously pleased. She exchanged a long, warm gaze with Tamra that was worth a thousand words.

Returning to the house, the remainder of the day was spent playing board games and eating leftovers from the previous evening, while Tamra gradually came to accept this new, more satisfying part of her background. When evening settled in, Brady asked, "So, now that Christmas is over, what are your plans?"

"Well, we're going out to dinner and the symphony tomorrow," Jess said. "And I think we probably should get a flight out on Thursday or Friday." He turned to Tamra, "If that's all right with you, of course."

"That would be fine," she said, feeling a mixture of emotions. While she longed to pursue this budding relationship with her father and stepmother, she had to admit that she missed Australia. In her heart it had truly become her home.

"We're planning to stop in Utah for a few days to see my sisters and some friends," Jess said, "and then in California for a couple of days where another sister lives. And then back to the great Down Under."

"Well, we're sure going to miss you," Brady said, reaching for Claudia's hand. "But it's been wonderful." His voice carried a hint of emotion. "I have to say that . . . well, I've had a lot of heartache to think of my children being raised with so many . . . challenges. But the time we've spent together has healed a large part of me. It's been so good just to spend time with you . . . and to see that you're doing so well."

"The feeling is mutual," Tamra admitted. "And it's not like this is really good-bye. We'll keep in touch and—"

"We'll be writing lots of letters," Claudia said.

"And the phone calls aren't as expensive as you might think," Jess said. "And one day you'll just have to come and visit us—the sooner the better."

"Well, we . . ." Brady hesitated and glanced at his wife.

"Just tell them," she said with a smile.

"We've talked about it," Brady said, "and we think we might actually be able to get there for the wedding."

"Really?" Tamra practically squealed with excitement, then she laughed. "Oh, that would be wonderful!"

In a sober tone, Jess said, "I have to say that . . . well, you must understand that the actual ceremony will be in the temple, and only Church members in good standing can attend. But we will be having a luncheon and a reception, and we would *love* to have you there. My parents would be thrilled to have you stay with them; there's plenty of room, and there's no point spending money on a hotel."

"It sounds wonderful," Claudia said. "We're long overdue for a vacation. We have some money put away, and . . . we just want to do it."

Tamra laughed again and they talked for an hour about when would be the best time for them to come, and what they should plan on seeing while they were there. The very idea of sharing the life she'd come to love in Australia with these people she had grown to love filled her with a joy that she wouldn't have thought possible when she'd arrived in this city last week. Jess flashed her a warm smile, and she felt certain he knew how thoroughly happy she felt at that moment.

Chapter Six

The following morning, Jess made a few calls and arranged their trip to Utah; their flight would be leaving Friday morning. They spent the day doing some more sightseeing around the city, and Jess insisted they return to the mall and ride the roller coaster again. He liked it so much that they rode it three times.

They stopped to see Brady and Claudia late that afternoon to say their farewells, since they would both be busy the following day. Brady had another inspection, and Claudia would be helping a friend all day. It was difficult to say good-bye, but Tamra left knowing that this was just the beginning of a lifelong relationship with two wonderful people that had not even existed for her last week.

It was more difficult to say good-bye to her grandmother. With the state of her health, Tamra doubted she would ever see Rayna alive again. But she reminded herself of how grateful she was to have known her at all.

In Tamra's opinion, dinner out and the symphony put the perfect finishing touches on a perfect week, and it was a great distraction from her good-byes earlier in the day. But lying in bed that night, she couldn't keep her thoughts from straying to her mother and brother. She came up with an idea that actually made her excited, and it took great self-control to not call Jess's room in the middle of the night and tell him. But the minute he came to get her the next morning for breakfast, she blurted out, "We need to go shopping again, and back to the copy center."

"We do?" he asked with a grin, obviously pleased with her enthusiasm.

"I want to get my mother and brother an early Christmas gift. I want to give my mother a book of genealogy for her side of the family. And . . . I don't know what to get my brother, but I'll think of something."

"Okay," Jess said, "let's go."

Getting the book ready for her mother was relatively simple, since they'd gone through the process only a few days earlier. But wandering around Target, Tamra couldn't begin to guess what her brother might like. She finally resorted to praying while they sat at the snack bar and had a sandwich. While she was sporadically scanning childhood memories to recall what she knew of her brother's personality, an idea sprang into her mind.

"I know what to get," she said brightly, and led Jess to the toy section. When they were standing in front of the Legos, she told him, "I remember Mel asking for Legos for Christmas five or six years in a row. But he never got any. Mother always told him they made too big of a mess and he didn't deserve them."

"That's terrible," Jess said, as if life without Legos was tantamount to living only on bread and water.

"Yes, I think it is," Tamra added. "For me it was an Easy-Bake Oven. I wanted one so badly, but she said it was a waste of money and I would make a mess. After a few years I quit asking. But I'm not going to think about that. It doesn't matter anymore. Still, I think Mel just might appreciate a good set of Legos. And if *you* still like to play with them, maybe he will too."

Jess rubbed his hands together with excitement. "Which set should we get? Star Wars? Harry Potter?"

"Nah, I think he would rather have something a little more . . . classic. How about this one?" She pointed to a castle set, complete with knights, horses, and a fire-breathing dragon.

"Perfect," Jess said and carried the box to the checkout counter.

Back at the motel, Tamra wrapped the gifts while Jess called his sister in Utah to let her know their plans. When the gifts were ready, they went straight to the bar, knowing this time of day would be the best to catch them without crowds. Tamra tried to talk herself out of being nervous, but she wanted this experience to put a more positive note on her relationship with Mel and her mother. And she prayed that it would go well.

Tamra took a deep breath and walked into the bar with Jess beside her. The scene they found was familiar, just as were the feelings rumbling inside her. Why did she have to feel this way about facing her own mother? Why did something so simple and ordinary to most people have to be such a tormenting ordeal for her?

Tamra pushed the questions aside and forced herself to the moment. As they moved closer to where her mother and Mel were talking quietly, they both glanced up, their expressions a combination of surprise and suspicion. Tamra saw their eyes move at the same time to the gifts she carried. Wanting to get this over as quickly as possible, she cleared her throat and hurried to set the packages on the bar.

"Hi," she said, "I just wanted to see you once more before we leave, and . . . since Christmas isn't far off, I thought I'd drop off some gifts." She hated the need to clarify. "I'm not expecting anything in return. I just wanted to leave these and . . ." She noticed Mel's expression softening, but her mother still looked skeptical.

Mel chuckled and asked, "Can I open it now?"

Tamra had planned on just leaving the gifts, but she said, "If you want to—sure."

Mel's face took on the expression of a delighted child as he carefully removed the bow and tore the paper away. Tamra felt a pang of heartache on his behalf. What were holidays like living and working with this cynical and belligerent woman? The holiday celebration she'd just experienced gave her some idea of all she'd missed out on in her life. But did Mel have any idea of that perspective?

His eyes showed a baffled amusement as the box of Legos came into view. He looked toward Tamra in question, and for the first time since her early childhood, she felt like his sister. It was easy to say, "You always wanted Legos for Christmas when we were kids. I don't know if you ever got any, but . . . well, Jess likes to play with Legos. I guess there are some things you're never too old to do."

Tamra stole a quick glance at her mother, relieved to see that her expression showed indifference. She wondered if Mel remembered, as she did, that his repeated requests for Legos had been callously disregarded by an insensitive mother. He looked at her again, with something soft showing in his eyes, and she felt certain that he did. "Thank you," he said, and she knew that he meant it.

"You're welcome," she said.

An awkward silence descended while Tamra considered how to make an exit. Mel interjected with a vibrant, "Open yours, Mom."

Tamra quickly added, "You don't have to right now if you don't want to or . . ." She stopped as Myrna carefully opened the gift. In response to her puzzled expression, Tamra explained, "Those are copies of the genealogical records of your ancestors. Your mother's line goes back to the early seventeenth century. I couldn't get back quite that far on your father's line." While Myrna thumbed through the pages, her face expressionless, Tamra added, "Your great-great-grandfather on your mother's side was the second son of an English Earl who had a hand in establishing the colony of Virginia." Following more silence, she concluded by saying, "I just thought you might be interested."

"Well, that's all very fascinating," Myrna said, subtly sarcastic as she closed the book abruptly. Tamra winced and took a step back, grateful to feel Jess's hand come to her shoulder. Myrna turned cold eyes on Tamra and said, "I think you'd better go now." While Tamra was too stunned to know how to respond, Myrna added, "I don't know what it is you're after, but you're not going to get it."

"I've told you," Tamra said, "I'm not after anything."

"And I should believe you? After you've come in here three times? You're obviously trying to—"

"It's just a gift, Mother," Tamra said, barely managing a steady voice. "I'm sorry we bothered you." She glanced toward her brother to see if his eyes showed some compassion for her, but he obviously had no intention of pointing out his mother's inappropriate behavior. Tamra turned to leave and Jess followed. She bit her tongue from tossing back one more cynical remark and forced herself to just go.

They said nothing as they walked to the car, but Jess kept his arm tightly about her shoulders. The drive back to the motel was equally silent, while Tamra felt as if a festering wound, deep inside her, was threatening to burst and leak toxic emotions into every crevice of her heart and soul. When they got out of the car at the motel, Tamra felt a sudden desperate need to have some time and space—a great deal of it. They were almost to the door of her room when she stopped and said, "Can I have the keys to the car?"

"What for?" Jess asked, sounding alarmed.

"I just need to . . . drive," she insisted.

"Where?" he asked, his panic increasing.

"I don't know *where*," she hissed. "I just need to get out of here."

"Okay," he said hesitantly, "but—"

"Just give me the keys!" she shouted.

Jess reluctantly lifted them up. "You're not going to do anything stupid, are you?"

"I told you," she snapped as she grabbed the keys, "I just need some time."

"You're not going to abandon me in this stupid motel, are you?" he called as she walked away. She only tossed him a glare and hurried to the car.

Jess watched her drive away, feeling the same kind of knots in his stomach that he'd felt when he'd gone home to find out that she'd left and no one knew where she'd gone. At the time, his fears had been intense and all consuming. And he felt that way now. He went into his room and got down on his knees, praying for her safety, and for her heart to be comforted and softened. When his prayer was finished, he called Brady and told him what had happened. He told Jess he'd call if he saw her, and Jess promised to do the same. Then Jess called Australia, oblivious to what time it might be on the other end of the world. He needed to talk to his parents.

* * *

Tamra drove through the city for hours. The sun set as she crossed the river for the fifth time. Every mile was accompanied by memories that stung and burned her spirit, while a steady stream of tears drizzled silently over her face. Almost unconsciously, she found herself at the care center where her grandmother was living. She found Rayna just being put into bed, but the nurse left them to visit. Tamra pulled a chair close to the bed and took her grandmother's frail hand. Rayna's eyes showed recognition and delight.

"You're probably thinking that we already said good-bye, and I wasn't supposed to come back, but . . . well, I know you must be tired, Grandma," she said, "but I need to talk. I hope you don't mind." Rayna's eyes clearly expressed her pleasure, and Tamra quickly spilled the torrent of her emotion and its greatest cause—the lack of love from her mother. When she had nothing more to say, she looked into her grandmother's eyes and could see the love this woman had for her. She pressed a kiss to the older woman's face and whispered, "I love you, Grandma, and I know you love me. I guess, somehow, everything will be all right." She leaned back and added, "Thanks for listening."

Rayna's eyes smiled again, but her fatigue was evident. Tamra stayed, holding her grandmother's hand until she drifted to sleep. She was startled to hear her father say, "I had a feeling you might show up here eventually." She looked up at him questioningly and he added, "I've checked here five times since Jess called me."

Tamra sighed and turned to look at her sleeping grandmother, if only to avoid facing her father. "He shouldn't have called; there's no need for you to worry."

"I'm glad he called," Brady said, quietly moving a chair close to hers. "We both love you and maybe we have cause to be worried." He took the hand that wasn't holding Rayna's. "Your mother is a bitter, difficult woman, Tamra. We don't know why, and it really doesn't matter. The only thing that matters is . . . well, we just have to make it stop—right here, right now. You can't control what she does or how she feels. But you have your whole life ahead of you, and you are stronger than either of your parents could ever dream of being."

Tamra hung her head. "I'm not so sure."

Brady lifted her chin, forcing her to look at him. "I am," he said. "Until you find that strength inside of you, you're just going to have to trust me when I tell you that everything you need in order to be happy is already within your reach. Take it, Tamra. Take all you've made of your life, and make the rest of your life everything that you deserve."

Even while she felt as if his words could never penetrate her clouded state of mind, she was overcome with a sudden rush of emotion and found her face pressed to his shoulder, her sobs muffled in the fabric of his coat. She reminded herself of all the blessings that had been poured out to compensate for the struggles of her life. She was truly blessed and she knew it. But she felt somehow unworthy of all she'd been given, and she just didn't know how to get past such feelings and find the strength and happiness her father was describing.

Her sobs quieted, and there were several minutes of peaceable silence until her father said, "You should get back to your room and get some sleep. I know you have an early flight."

He urged her to her feet and she said, "I don't want to say good-bye again."

"Then don't say it," he said. "Just go. I told you before, we'll keep in touch, and we just might make it for the wedding. This isn't the end of our relationship, Tamra; it's the beginning." She managed a smile. He kissed her cheek and repeated, "Just go. Don't look back. Take hold of your future and don't look back."

"I love you, Dad," Tamra said and eased away from him.

"I love you, too," he said in a voice that cracked, and Tamra hurried from the room.

* * *

Jess abruptly halted his pacing when the phone rang. "It's Brady," he heard after he'd answered. "I found her with my mother. She's on her way back . . . provided she doesn't take any detours. Will you call and let me know when she gets there? No matter how late."

"I will," Jess said, "and thank you."

"Be patient with her, Jess," Brady said. "The way Claudia was with me."

"The way Tamra was with *me*," Jess said. "She's everything to me, Brady. I've got forever."

About twenty minutes after he hung up the phone, Jess heard a car outside and looked between the drapes to see that it was Tamra. Relief crept through his entire being. He grabbed his coat and stepped outside as she approached, needing to pass his door to get to her own. She looked startled but not surprised.

"You okay?" he asked, relieved to have her put the keys in his hand.

"I will be, I suppose," she said and stepped past him. "We should get some sleep."

"I love you, Tamra," Jess said.

She inhaled sharply and cast him a brief, intense gaze. "I love you too, Jess. Wake me in time to get packed."

He nodded. "I'll see you in the morning."

Jess waited until she went into her room and he heard her turn the deadbolt. He returned to his own room and gave Brady a quick call, then he attempted to sleep even though his entire soul over-flowed with concern for this woman he loved. He knew all too well what it was like to hurt over circumstances that felt beyond your control. All he could do was be there for her, and pray that she would be able to take hold of the same healing power that had carried him beyond his darkest hours.

* * *

Tamra was deeply relieved to feel the plane rise into the air, putting distance between herself and the unpleasant associations of this city. But she felt great sorrow at leaving behind her grandmother, wondering if they would ever see each other again in this life. And she ached to hold onto the budding relationship she had found with her father and stepmother. She reminded herself that long-distance rela-tionships were easy to maintain in this electronic age. But still, she missed them already, and prayed it wouldn't be too long before they could see each other again.

Jess's presence in the seat next to her assuaged her rumbling emotions. His hand slipped into hers and she wished she could tell him what his silent, nonquestioning attitude meant to her. They had exchanged no words beyond those necessary since they'd set out for the airport. But she sensed his love and support, and he seemed to know that she needed some time and space to think through all she'd encountered during their visit to her hometown.

Tamra drifted to sleep and awoke to discover that they were more than halfway to Utah. As Jess talked about his excitement in being able to see his sisters, her mind turned more to the path ahead, rather than the one she was leaving behind. *Don't look back,* she heard her father say in her memory. And with his words, she felt his love. And yes, it *did* ease the pain from the lack of warmth she'd gotten from her mother. She had to keep her perspective. Still, she couldn't deny the constant ache hovering inside of her. And while she longed to be free of it, she simply didn't know if such a thing was possible. But she forced her mind to anticipate their arrival in Utah, and she concen-trated on the feel of Jess's hand in hers. She had to believe that every-thing would be all right.

* * *

They arrived in Salt Lake City after dark and rented a car. The minute they stepped out into the night air, Jess commented, "It's not nearly as cold here as it is in Minnesota, thank heaven."

"Wimp," Tamra teased, and Jess readily pleaded guilty

Driving away from the airport, Jess said, "Now I know my way around in *this* city."

Tamra smiled, knowing he'd served his mission in this area, and he'd gotten most of his education not far from here at BYU. From the freeway Tamra could see the spires of the Salt Lake Temple shining brilliantly amidst the high-rises of the city.

"It's so beautiful," she commented, wondering why she felt sad.

"We'll come back before we leave the state," Jess said, "when we're not so tired, and you can explore the Square to your heart's content."

"Sounds wonderful."

"And," he drawled, "I was thinking . . . if you're interested—I would really like to go to the temple and do a session while we're here." He glanced toward her and added, "It's been too dreadfully long for me, and I just . . . want to."

"That sounds *especially* wonderful," she said.

Tamra dozed off and on throughout the hour's drive to Provo, wondering why she felt so tired. Jet lag, perhaps. After getting a quick supper, they checked into their separate motel rooms and Tamra fell quickly asleep.

The following day, Jess brought a breakfast tray to Tamra's room from the daily buffet that was included with the price of the room. While they were eating he announced that his quest for the day was to get the things he'd left behind when he'd left Utah abruptly several months ago. He wanted to sort through his things, box them up appropriately and ship them to Australia. "The hard part," he said, "is that they are in Heather's parents' garage."

Tamra felt a little taken aback. Heather was the woman Jess had once been in love with. She had waited for him on his mission, but their plans to marry had been put off by the accident that had nearly killed Jess. And Tamra knew that the entire matter was complicated by the fact that just prior to the accident, Heather had admitted to

Jess that she was uncertain about their relationship, and she had feelings for Jess's best friend, Byron—who had been killed in the accident. Jess had told Tamra that Heather was a good woman and she had never been dishonest with him or flaky. They had tried to put their relationship back together once Jess had healed from the accident. But it had slowly dwindled and he'd returned to Australia when she had told him she was marrying another man. Tamra felt confident that Jess's feelings for Heather were long in the past. Still, she had to ask, "Why is that hard?" When he didn't answer, she wondered if she had any cause for concern. She came right out and asked, "You don't still have feelings for her that—"

"No, of course not," he said. "It's just . . . Well, I don't think her parents were very happy about our relationship not working out. They're good people, and they had no problem with my leaving some things there, but . . . I'll just be glad to have this over. I really should have taken them to my sister's place."

"So, let's just do it. We should call and make sure they'll be there."

"My thoughts exactly," he said. "And if you don't mind, I'm going to have *you* call." He set the phone on the table beside her.

"And what exactly did you want me to say?" she asked, feeling a little chagrined, but not enough to protest. He'd held her hand through a great deal of drama with her family; surely she could call Heather's parents.

"Just say that you're calling for me, and you wondered if we could stop by and get my things. Simple as that." He dialed the number from memory and handed her the receiver.

"What's their last name?" she asked while it was ringing.

"Behunin," he said and she quickly repeated it to make sure she had it.

A woman answered and Tamra asked, "Is this Mrs. Behunin?"

"Uh, no . . . they're on a mission. This is their daughter. May I help you?"

"I hope so. My name is Tamra Banks. I'm calling for Jess Hamilton. We're in town and I was wondering when we might come by and get the things he left there."

"Any time today would be fine," she said. "I'm not going anywhere until after six."

"Great," Tamra said.

She was surprised to be asked, "By *we,* do you mean Jess is coming with you?"

She hesitated only a moment before she said, "He's the one who knows how to get there."

Jess furrowed his brow, as if he was trying to figure out the conversation.

"Okay," the woman said, "I'll see you later, then."

"Thank you," Tamra said and hung up the phone.

"What?" Jess asked.

"They're on a mission. That was their daughter."

"*Which* daughter?" he demanded.

"How should I know? What was I supposed to say? '*Which one are you?*'"

"Sorry," Jess said. "There's a fifty-fifty chance that Heather is the daughter house-sitting while her parents are away."

"And even if she's not, I'd wager her sister is calling her right now to tell her you're coming."

Jess sighed and Tamra said, "Let's just go get it over with."

Driving through Provo in daylight brought back memories for Tamra of going to the MTC here at the beginning of her mission. Jess didn't say much, but she left him to his thoughts. He drove into a middle-class neighborhood and parked in front of a red brick home with a couple of huge maple trees in the yard.

Jess turned off the engine, then just sat there. "Just do it, Jess," said Tamra. "Maybe it would be better if it *was* Heather. She's not going to bite you or anything. And if she tries, I'll protect you."

This made him laugh, and he got out of the car. She sensed his nervousness as he pressed the doorbell. The door came open quickly and Tamra knew it was Heather simply by the way they both stood momentarily stunned. Tamra couldn't help appraising her since she was the woman who had once been a significant part of Jess's life. What surprised Tamra was the stark evidence that this woman was so unlike herself. Her blonde hair was cut extremely short. She wore a great deal of makeup and several pieces of jewelry, even though she was dressed casually. She was several inches shorter than Tamra, and obviously pregnant.

"Hello," she finally said.

"Hello," Jess replied.

"How are you?" she asked.

"I'm great," he said. "How are you?"

"Good," she said with a sincere smile. "It's good to see you."

"And you," he said.

Heather's eyes moved to Tamra. "And is this your secretary who called me this morning?"

Jess gave an embarrassed chuckle. "I thought your parents might not have been very happy to hear from me."

"They knew it were for the best, Jess—we all did." Her tone was cautious, as if she were testing his attitude.

Jess responded with an eager, "Yes, it certainly was. And this is *not* my secretary. This is Tamra Banks—my fiancée."

"Oh?" Heather said, seeming pleased. "How nice."

"It's a pleasure to meet you, Heather," Tamra said, extending a hand.

"Likewise," Heather said, shaking it eagerly. "You're American."

"Only by birth," Tamra said. Jess looked as surprised as Heather. She added, "I think I'm Australian at heart."

"Well," Heather said, stepping out onto the porch and leading the way to the garage, "things are obviously going well."

"Yes, they are," Jess said.

"Your parents made it home safely, I take it," she said.

"Yes, and yours are off serving, I hear."

"Yes, they're in New York. Jeremy and I are staying here while they're gone, which works out nicely since he's finishing up his degree at the Y."

Heather opened the garage door and pointed to a stack of boxes against the wall, amidst a neatly organized array of stored items. "It's all right there," she said. "If you need to sort anything or . . . whatever, take your time."

"Actually, that would be great," Jess said. "I think some of this stuff can go to DI or some charity, and I want to get the rest shipped off."

Heather asked Tamra a couple of questions about herself while Jess pulled the boxes down and opened each one.

"Need some help?" Tamra asked.

"Not at the moment," he said. "Some advice, perhaps. Most of this stuff is probably not worth what it would cost to ship it. Maybe you can keep me from being a sentimental fool."

After a few minutes of growing tension, while Jess rummaged through an odd array of things, Heather said, "You know, Jess, there's something I have to ask you, and I'm going to hate myself if I don't take advantage of your being here to do it, but . . ." She glanced briefly toward Tamra. "Perhaps it would be more appropriate to discuss it privately."

Jess straightened his back and looked at Heather skeptically. "I have no secrets from Tamra," he said, but Tamra could see the tension in his eyes.

Not certain if he would prefer to have her there or gone, she said, "I can just take a little walk. You won't hurt my feelings or anything if—"

"You're just fine," Jess said with a long gaze. Then his eyes turned to Heather. "What is it?"

"Well." Heather seemed suddenly nervous. "I have to say that, first of all, I'm glad to see that you're doing so well. I've been terribly worried about you since . . . Well, I know when you left here, not long before the wedding, you weren't doing well. And you know I had no doubt that marrying Jeremy was the right thing, but . . . as I said, I've been worried, especially since I'd heard that . . ." She glanced down and cleared her throat tensely. She looked back at Jess and asked in a shaky voice, "Jess, I have to know. Was I the reason you tried to kill yourself?"

Tamra gasped audibly before she put a hand over her mouth. The shock in Jess's expression was evident, but she had no idea how he was feeling. Heather glanced toward Tamra before she said, "I hope you meant it when you said you had no secrets, because I wouldn't want her to learn such a thing from me."

"She knows everything," Jess said in an even voice, but something subtly angry showed in his eyes. "What I want to know is how *you* found out about something that was absolutely none of your business."

"After all that you and I had been through together, your being hospitalized in the psychiatric ward certainly *was* my business. I had good reason to be concerned."

"How?" he demanded. The muscles in his face tightened.

"I called the house to see how you were doing. Sadie said you were in the hospital, but she wouldn't tell me anything. I called the hospital, but they wouldn't tell me anything so I . . . well, I told them I was your sister, and I gave them enough information about you that they believed me. I wouldn't blame you for being angry with me, but I had to know." Her voice softened and she asked, "Why, Jess? Why would you do something like that? If you had succeeded, do you think I would have ever been able to live with it?"

"I should hope so," he said, "because it had nothing to do with you. Even if you had left me high and dry—which you didn't—it was my decision to do what I did. No one had accountability in that choice but me."

Heather sighed audibly, as if his words had eased her anxiety significantly. But there was an edge to her voice as she said, "Forgive me, Jess, but this has been hard for me. I have to admit I've been terribly angry, and I've barely kept myself from calling and telling you so a number of times. I just don't understand how you could do something so . . . *selfish*."

Jess said to Tamra, "She sounds a lot like you. It would seem the two of you have a lot in common."

Heather looked confused but apparently chose to ignore the comment. "Why?" she asked. "I don't understand."

"Well, I can't answer that, Heather." His expression softened with his voice. "I have trouble figuring it out myself. I think I just let all that pain and fear get the better of me, instead of trusting in the Lord to help me get past it."

"Was it the accident?"

"Mostly, yes," he said.

"And now?" she asked. "Have you been able to get past it?"

"Yes, I have," he said earnestly while he shared a lingering glance with Tamra.

"Well, that's wonderful, then," Heather said. She added, more to Tamra, "Forgive the dramatics, Miss Banks. It was something I had to know."

"I understand," Tamra said. "If I were in your place, I likely would have done the same."

"Well." Heather smiled, seeming immensely more relaxed. "I'm glad he's found someone who can appreciate what an incredible man he is." She turned to Jess and added, "So, how is it exactly that we have a lot in common?"

"She told me I was selfish too," he said almost lightly.

"You mean . . . you knew each other before . . ." She glanced between them, seeming confused. "But didn't it happen soon after you went home?"

"That's right," Jess said.

"So, the two of you met . . . ?"

"Right after I got home," he said.

"So," she said, turning to Tamra, "obviously you knew he was in the hospital when—"

"She *put* me in the hospital," Jess said. "She's the one who found me."

Heather searched his expression as if to question his sincerity, then she turned to Tamra, her expression a mixture of surprise and gratitude. Without saying a word, she hugged Tamra tightly then stepped back and wiped tears from her face. "Let me know if you need anything. I'll be in the kitchen," she said, and hurried back to the house.

Chapter Seven

Jess turned to look at Tamra for a long moment before he returned to his chore, as if he simply didn't know what to say.

It only took Jess another twenty minutes to sort through his things. He sent Tamra to the car for a marker and some packing tape that he'd brought along. He taped and addressed two small boxes to be shipped to his home, which he put in the backseat. And everything else was put into the trunk to be donated to Deseret Industries.

"Did you get your boots?" Tamra asked as he closed the garage. How well she remembered him buying riding boots soon after she'd met him, since he'd left his well-loved pair in Utah.

"Yes," he said, smiling. "I got my boots."

They went back to the door where Heather met them before Jess could ring the bell. "Thank you," he said, "for everything."

She smiled and said, "No problem." Turning to Tamra, she said, "It was truly a pleasure to meet you, Tamra." Heather hugged her again. "It might sound funny, but . . . I think I can be happier knowing that he's happy."

"It was nice meeting you, as well," said Tamra. "And if he's half as happy as I am, he'll be fine, I can assure you."

Heather smiled and turned to Jess. She hugged him quickly and said, "I'm glad you came, Jess. It was an answer to my prayers, I believe."

"Keep in touch," he said. "You know my address."

They drove away from Heather's home in silence. It was several minutes before Jess said, "That has got to be one of the strangest experiences of my life, beyond realizing I'd almost killed myself."

"What?" Tamra asked.

"To stand there and watch you and Heather talking about me like that, and then you *hugged* each other. It's almost like one of those dreams you have that's so weird you're glad it was a dream when you wake up."

"Most people call that a nightmare."

"It wasn't scary; it was just weird."

"Are you glad you saw her?" Tamra asked.

"Yes, actually, I am. It's pretty humiliating to think of her knowing . . . what I did. But since she *did* know, I can understand why she would need some closure."

"And how are *you*? Do you have closure?"

He glanced toward her then back to the road. "Over Heather or attempting suicide?"

"Both."

"Yes, I believe I do."

"Good," she said. "Now you can take me to lunch. I want to go to your favorite place to eat while you were going to school here."

"Oh, that's easy," he said and did a U-turn. He took her to a place called Brick Oven and ordered pizza and apple beer.

After lunch they stopped at the post office and Deseret Industries, then Tamra asked, "Now what? You've accomplished your quest for the day, and the day's not over yet."

"Well, I'm anxious to see my sisters, but no one's going to be home until later this afternoon. There are a couple of other visits I'd like to make, but they don't know I'm coming, so I don't know if anyone will be around this time of day."

"So, take me sightseeing until they're around."

"Well, I'm going to make one try since we're not far away, and if he's not available, we'll go sightseeing."

"Okay. Who are we going to see?"

"Sean."

"Your sort-of foster brother?"

"That's him."

"The one you talked to on the phone that . . . helped so much," she stated, remembering his role in Jess's emotional and spiritual recovery.

"That's him," Jess repeated more earnestly.

"I can't wait to meet him."

Tamra's mind wandered to the weeks and months of praying for Jess to come to terms with his pain and get on with his life. When he'd finally left home, she had feared she'd never see him again. But she'd learned later that he had called Sean O'Hara from a motel room, and their lengthy conversation had spurred Jess to turn to his Father in Heaven and apply the Atonement in his life in a way he'd never considered before.

Jess had told Tamra that Sean had been taken in by his family when they'd lived in Provo for a few years during Jess's childhood. Sean had been living on his own, going to BYU, and having some personal challenges—although Tamra couldn't recall exactly what they might have been.

They pulled up in front of an older home that had been renovated into offices. Jess led her into the lobby of the little office with Sean O'Hara's name on the door. He said to the woman behind the desk, "Is the good doctor with a client?"

"Yes," she said, "but he should be done in about twenty minutes. Is there something I can help you with?"

"You certainly can," he said. "As soon as his client leaves, just tell him there's a hysterical man threatening suicide out here, and I promise to not keep him too long."

The woman smiled slyly and said, "I'll tell him."

"In the meantime," he said, "I'll read the jokes in the *Reader's Digest*."

Jess found the magazine and read the jokes aloud to Tamra for about fifteen minutes before a woman came out of a door and left the office after exchanging some friendly small talk with the woman behind the desk. After she was gone, a man came out the same door; he reminded Tamra somehow of Jess, except that they looked nothing alike. It was perhaps simply the way he dressed and carried himself. Without glancing toward the waiting room, he leaned over the receptionist's desk and said, "Have I got a few minutes now to—"

"You do have a little time," she said, "once you deal with the hysterical man threatening suicide." She pointed at Jess with her pencil.

Without turning around, Sean O'Hara said, "He wouldn't happen to have an Australian accent, would he?"

The receptionist chuckled. "I do believe he would," she said, and Sean turned to look over his shoulder.

His face broke into a grin. He turned and put his hands on his hips. "How on earth did you get here?"

"Well, you see," Jess said, "we got on a plane." He made flying noises and moved his hand through the air to demonstrate. "It flew over the ocean to L.A. and we got on another plane." More plane noises. "And we went to Minneapolis, spent some time there, then we flew," he made a whooshing sound, "to Salt Lake City and," he made car noises, "we drove down I-15. And here we are."

"Sorry I asked," Sean said and stepped toward them. Jess rose to his feet and they both laughed as they embraced and slapped each other's shoulders.

"It's so good to see you," Sean said and laughed again. "And you look good. You doing okay, or did you come for a shrink session?"

"I'm fine," he said, "but this woman here . . ." He motioned toward Tamra, who was still sitting. He whispered loudly while he smirked at Tamra. "Just between you and me, I think she's crazy. She actually said she would marry me."

Tamra laughed and came to her feet. "Well then," Sean said, extending a hand, "you and I need to have a little talk. Do you have any idea what you're getting yourself into?"

"I believe I do," she said, then added a little too seriously, "Perhaps Jess is the one who is crazy. I don't think he knows what *he's* in for."

Her tone of voice and the intensity in her eyes left Jess feeling mildly alarmed. He wanted to demand what she meant by that, but Sean smiled and added, "You must be Tamra. I've heard great things about you."

"And I've heard great things about *you*," she said. "It's nice to meet you face-to-face so I can tell you how much I appreciate everything you said to Jess. He told me how much you helped him. I think you were the answer to many prayers."

Sean offered a humble smile. "It's like I told Jess; I was just the messenger."

"Well, thank you for having the right message." She reached out and took Jess's hand as if nothing were wrong. But looking closely into her eyes, Jess caught a subtle, but unmistakable, doubt.

"So, how long will you be in town?" Sean asked.

"A few days, I guess," Jess said. "We don't have any specific plans beyond seeing my sisters."

"Well then," Sean said, "we must all go out to dinner before you leave."

"Sounds great," Jess said, then he asked how Sean's family was doing. They chatted for several minutes, exchanging small talk and catching up. Then Sean glanced at his watch and said, "Listen, I need to get back to work. But I'll call Allie later and we'll make some plans."

"Sounds great," Jess said.

"It was nice meeting you," Tamra said.

"And you," Sean replied with a smile.

The moment they stepped outside, Jess said, "What's wrong, Tamra?"

"I'm just a little tired, why?"

"That's not what I mean," he said and she glared at him. He opened the car door for her then went around and got in, but he didn't put the key in the ignition. "I know you well enough to know that something's wrong."

Tamra attempted to look baffled, but when his intense gaze seemed to see right through her, she turned abruptly toward the window.

"You're hiding something from me, and I know it. Ever since that last visit with your mother, something's been bugging you. I figured you just needed some space and time, so I've given it to you. But I need to know why you so adamantly insist that I'm crazy and I don't know what I'm in for. Is there some dark secret about you that you haven't told me? A satanic cult, perhaps?"

"Don't be ridiculous!"

"If I don't know what I'm in for, then you'd better tell me."

Tamra sighed heavily. "There's nothing to tell you that you don't already know."

"Then apparently I *do* know what I'm in for."

"Do you?" she countered. "When it comes to the reality of raising children and coping with whatever may come up, do you have any idea of how my upbringing may affect our lives? You were raised by good, honest people who expressed love and commitment and worked through their problems effectively. I was raised with yelling and screaming, foul language and *abuse*. How do you know that the effects of my abuse aren't still lingering somewhere down inside of me? How do you know I don't have problems that could surface and end up coming between us?"

Jess turned in his seat and leaned toward her. "And how do you know that I won't hit a mid-life crisis and become suicidal again? You don't know that my problems won't affect your life, any more than I know that your problems won't affect mine. But I'll tell you what I *do* know. I know that we are supposed to be together, and with the commitment we share and applying the gospel in our lives, we can work through anything—*anything!* Are you hearing me?" he asked, but she only turned further away. He softened his voice and went on. "Listen, Tam, I can understand why these encounters with your mother were difficult. I can understand how ugly memories have been dredged up, and it can't be easy having a mother treat you the way she does. But I think you're losing perspective here. You're losing sight of how strong and resilient your spirit is, how far you've come in *spite* of your upbringing."

His voice softened further, and he put a hand on her arm. "Tamra, you're the one who taught me that the Atonement paid the price for my suffering, and my weaknesses, and I didn't have to carry that burden. Is it so hard for you to apply the same principles to your own life?"

Tamra snapped her head toward him, her eyes hot. "Maybe it is," she said, more sad than angry.

When she said nothing more, Jess took her hand and pleaded, "Talk to me, Tamra. Don't shut me out the way you used to get angry with me for doing."

Tamra sighed. "So, what? Now you're calling me a hypocrite?"

"I didn't say that."

"You implied it," she snapped.

"And your defensiveness implies that you must be feeling like a hypocrite," he stated calmly.

Tamra sighed again and hung her head. "Maybe I do."

"Just talk to me."

Jess waited while silent tears spilled down her cheeks. She wiped them away with her free hand before she said, "I don't know what's wrong. If I could pinpoint it, maybe I could find a way to feel better. I mean . . . the experiences with my dad, and my grandmother, were . . . well, they were wonderful. I'm grateful for that. And I think it helped me gain some perspective. But . . ."

"But?" he pressed when she hesitated.

"I just can't get rid of this uneasiness I feel about my mother."

"So . . . define uneasiness. What kind of uneasiness?"

"I don't know. I just feel . . . confused, angry sometimes, horribly sad at other times. And maybe I just feel sorry for myself. I can't help wondering why I had to endure such a horrible childhood, and why I can't have a mother who is the slightest bit decent."

Jess blew out a long breath. "I can't answer those questions, Tamra. I can only remind you of how much you *do* have."

"Yes, I have been very blessed, Jess. I know that. But sometimes that makes me feel even worse. I look at all I've been given, and I wonder why I have to feel this way over this one issue. I almost feel like a spoiled child, saying, 'I know I have *almost* everything I could ever want, but I won't be happy until I have it *all*.'"

"I don't see it that way," Jess said. "I know all too well how feelings over one issue in your life can make the rest of your life difficult."

Tamra turned to look at him. "And perhaps I have some degree of understanding of what you went through." She sighed and touched his face. "From the outside, it seemed so easy; I kept thinking if you would just turn it over to the Lord and let go, you could be free of your burden. But it's not that easy, is it?"

"Not easy, perhaps, but it is that simple. You *do* need to turn it over to the Lord, Tamra, and trust Him to guide you to the answers."

Tears came again as Tamra admitted, "But sometimes I feel so . . . unworthy; unworthy of His blessings . . . of your love for me . . . of all that I've been given, and . . ."

Jess urged her head to his shoulder as she became upset. "It's not true, Tamra. I've heard those same thoughts in my own head, and I know well enough where such thoughts come from. Satan's working to convince you that you are unworthy of the very blessings that can lift you out of your suffering. You're an incredible woman, and God loves you." He eased back and looked into her eyes, "I love you too. And you *are* worthy . . . of all you've been blessed with and more."

She gave him a wan smile, but he could see in her eyes that she didn't completely believe him. He told himself that it would take time to convince her. But he had forever. She had stood by him through his own internal struggles. And he would do the same for her—no matter how long it took.

"Hey," she said, an abrupt change in her voice, "you promised to show me around the city. I think now would be a good time."

Jess turned the key in the ignition and pulled onto the road, praying in his heart that she would get beyond this and be able to see herself the way he saw her. He just had to believe that with time, she would.

* * *

Tamra enjoyed Jess's tour of the BYU campus. And driving past the Provo temple and the MTC brought back many memories. She especially enjoyed their drive through the neighborhood where he had lived through part of his childhood while his mother, Emily, had been going to BYU. And not far from that house was the one where his mother had lived when she'd been married to her first husband. His half-sisters, Allison, Amee, and Alexa, were from that first marriage, and they had been living in this house when Jess's father, Michael, had come back into Emily's life and had subsequently married her and taken her and her daughters to Australia. Jess was the oldest of Michael's and Emily's children, followed by James, who had been killed in the accident, along with his wife. Emma was Jess's only full-blooded sibling living, and was living here in Provo with Allison's family while she attended BYU. Emma had been born while the family lived in Utah, and her twin brother, Tyson, had died soon after birth.

Tamra appreciated seeing the neighborhood where so many significant events had happened in this family she was becoming a part of. She marveled at the challenges Michael and Emily had endured, and found that it helped give her some of that perspective she was seeking.

Jess pulled the car up in front of the house next door to where Emily had once lived with her first husband. Going toward the front door, he explained that Bret and Penny were some of his parents' dearest friends, and he couldn't come here without stopping to introduce them to his fiancée. Tamra enjoyed their brief visit, and she appreciated hearing some stories about Jess's family from a viewpoint she'd never heard before.

When they left to go to Allison's home, Tamra felt especially tired. Certain that the jet lag and strange hours she'd been keeping were catching up with her, she felt sure that a good night's sleep would put her right. She was tempted to ask Jess if she could go back to her motel room and take a nap, but she knew how excited he was to see his sisters. She'd simply go to bed early once they had a chance to visit.

Jess pulled the car into a wide driveway outside a beautiful home of rock and stucco. It was large without being ostentatious. Jess had barely stepped out of the car when his sister, Emma, came running out of the house. Just as the last time Tamra had seen them greet each other, Emma literally took a flying leap into his arms, and Jess easily caught her. They laughed and spun around together. Tamra didn't wait for Jess to open her door. She got out of the car and walked toward them just as his oldest sister, Allison, came running out of the house and embraced him with less drama. Emma turned toward Tamra and embraced her eagerly. "It's so good to see you again!" Emma announced and laughed again.

"And you," Tamra admitted readily. She'd almost forgotten how much she'd grown to love Jess's sisters in the brief time they'd spent together during their last visit to Australia. Allison turned and greeted Tamra with equal enthusiasm, and Tamra felt a warm layer of affirmation settling into place. She truly did have much to be grateful for. She had been taken into this wonderful family, and she had the hope of a bright future ahead of her with Jess. If only she could be free of this nagging uneasiness about her mother!

They went together into the house where Tamra met Allison's five children, who had all recently come in from school. Their dark skin and hair made her realize that their father must be dark. She vaguely recalled seeing pictures of the family once, but she'd forgotten. She figured it would take time to learn their names and keep track of them. While they were sitting in the family room visiting, Allison's husband, Ammon, came in from work. He was tall and dark, as she'd expected, though Tamra couldn't discern exactly what his ethnic background might be. He greeted Jess with laughter and a hearty embrace, then he greeted Tamra warmly when they were introduced. He sat to visit with them and she learned that he was co-owner of a successful construction company. Through the conversation Tamra learned that Ammon was a mixture of four different races, which explained his unique—and blatantly handsome—appearance.

Tamra's enjoyment of her visit began to wane when a subtle ache crept into her muscles. She was startled when the subtlety vanished instantly and she heard herself moan involuntarily.

"What's wrong?" Jess demanded, startling her again as the sound of his voice ground painfully through her head.

"I don't know," she muttered, unconsciously leaning her head against his shoulder. "I just hurt . . . all of a sudden."

Jess put a hand to her face. "Good heavens, girl. You're burning up. When did this come on?"

"I felt fine a few minutes ago," she said, "although I've been kind of . . . tired today."

"We need to get you to bed," Allison said.

"I don't want to be any bother," Tamra insisted. "If I could just—"

"Oh, for heaven's sake," Allison said, reminding Tamra of this woman's mother. "You're family. And even if you weren't, you're sick. Jess," she ordered, "go put her to bed."

"*Which* bed?" he asked, urging Tamra to her feet with his arm around her.

"*My* bed," Emma said.

"Where will *you* sleep?" Tamra asked without much conviction. "I don't want anyone else to get sick or—"

"We've dealt with sick people before," Allison declared. "We'll get out the Lysol spray and vitamin C and wash our hands and we'll manage just fine. You only need to worry about getting some rest."

Emma said to Jess, "Put her in my bed. I'll sleep in the top bunk, and I can keep an eye on her."

Tamra was so grateful to feel a bed beneath her that she couldn't find the will to protest the tender care she was getting. She could see now that she was in a bottom bunk in a room that was obviously Emma's.

While Jess removed her shoes and tucked her in, she heard Allison telling him to go to the motel and get their things. "It's silly for you to be renting rooms when we have plenty of space here."

"We didn't want to put you out or—"

Allison interrupted him. "You're family," she scolded. "And Tamra needs to be here where we can take care of her. Now go get her things so she can be comfortable."

"Yes, ma'am," he said with light sarcasm. "You're a lot like your mother, you know."

"I can think of no greater compliment," Allison said. "Now get going." She added, "Emma, get her some apple juice and some Tylenol. I'm going to call the doctor and see what kind of flu symptoms are going around."

Emma said to Tamra, "Does apple juice sound okay? Or do you want something else?"

"That sounds fine," Tamra said, amazed at how weak she felt. "Thank you."

"Are you hungry?" Emma added. "Do you want anything to—"

"No, I'll be fine. Thanks."

After the Tylenol kicked in, Tamra fell asleep and woke to find the room dimly lit from a lamp burning low on a desk across the room. Jess was sitting in a chair near the bed, reading out of the *Ensign*. When he saw that she was awake, he pressed a hand to her face. "You're getting warm again. I'll get you some more Tylenol."

"Thank you," Tamra said.

Allison and Emma returned with Jess and the Tylenol. Together they informed her that the body aches and weakness were typical of a nasty flu going around. Any other symptoms were mild, but the aches were reportedly horrible, and it would likely have her down for more than a week. Tamra groaned and apologized for upsetting the household, but Allison and Emma both assured her they were glad she'd waited to get sick until she'd gotten where they could take care of her. Their declarations that they were glad to be there for her were obviously genuine, and she felt grateful.

Tamra was shown to the bathroom that was off of Emma's room, then she was left to put on her pajamas that were among the things Jess had gathered from her motel room. When she was settled back into bed, Jess pointed out the nursery monitor close to her bed. Allison kept it around for when she had sick children who might need her help. Jess would keep the other part of it with him and be able to hear her if she needed anything.

"Thank you," she said, sinking more deeply into her pillow. "I guess we won't be making it home as soon as we'd expected."

"That's okay," Jess smiled and pressed a kiss to her brow.

"Careful," she said, "I don't want you getting sick."

"I'll be careful. And you just rest. We'll take good care of you."

"So, what are you going to do with yourself while I'm being a blob?" she asked.

"I'm going to do what I would be doing if I were home. I'm going to get online and get caught up on my schoolwork—and I'm going to take care of you. And I talked to my parents. They're working on wedding plans, and we'll deal with anything else after we get home."

Tamra sighed and silently thanked God for seeing that she was cared for. Then she drifted back to sleep.

For Tamra, the next several days went by in a blur of chills and sweating, drifting in and out of sleep at odd hours, and briefly interacting with those who came to check on her and see that her needs were met. Her only distinct memory was the priesthood blessing given to her the second day. When Jess and Ammon had both put their hands on her head, she'd felt warm and comforted. While it was evident she would be miserable for several days, she knew that all would be well.

Her sleep was often filled with strange dreams. More than once, she dreamt she was back in the Philippines, suffering from a fever that had been much more severe. Michael and Emily had been there to help her through, and now she was surrounded by their children and grandchildren, each showing love and concern in their own way. Jess was never far away, often doing his studies at Emma's computer just across the room from where she lay, day in and day out.

As the illness wore on, her dreams became more bizarre. She dreamt more than once that she was standing at the rail of the race track at Byrnehouse-Davies in Australia. Tamra had been able to see the track from her bedroom window in the Hamilton home, and she knew it had been there more than a century. And in her dreams she felt as if the track were new and the people surrounding her were dressed in Victorian-era clothing. While she cheered for the horses racing, a man put his hand on her shoulder and told her everything would be all right because he knew that Alexa would win the race. Memories of the dream clung with Tamra long after she awoke, and she reasoned that the man standing beside her had been Jess Davies, Jess's great-great-grandfather. She'd read the story in Alexa's journal of how she had won the race that saved Jess Davies' home; and she had also won his heart. Tamra drifted back to sleep and dreamt that an older Alexa was sitting beside the bed, checking her brow for fever. The following day she recalled reading in Jess's grandmother's journal of how she'd become ill in a strange town with nowhere to go, and Alexa had taken her in. Tamra liked the idea that perhaps Alexa was looking out for her now from the other side of the veil. Whether she was or not, it was still a nice thought.

Chapter Eight

Nine days after she became ill, Tamra awoke and felt different. It took her a few minutes to realize that the aching had relented and the fever had broken. She took a shower, which left her exhausted but definitely feeling free of the illness that had plagued her. She had barely laid back down when Jess came to check on her.

"How're you doing?" he asked, sitting on the edge of the bed.

"Better, actually," she said. "More weak than anything."

"Well, that's understandable," he said, kissing her brow.

"Did anyone else get sick?" she asked, feeling as if her mind were fully coherent for the first time in days.

"Not even a sniffle," he said with a smile, and she let out a slow sigh.

"How are the studies going?" she asked, slipping her hand into his.

"Quite well, actually. I got completely caught up and then some. So now that you're feeling better, we can enjoy the holiday and—"

"What holiday?" she demanded, lifting her head to look at him more directly.

"Thanksgiving is the day after tomorrow," he said.

"Really?" she asked dubiously and he chuckled.

"Really," he repeated. "And Allison's made it abundantly clear that we're not going anywhere until the first of the week. She's got big plans—all contingent on how you feel, of course. It's going to take some time to get your strength back."

Through a moment of silence, a thought occurred to Tamra. "Would we be celebrating Thanksgiving if we were in Australia? It is an American holiday, after all."

"We certainly would," he said. "Thanksgiving is one of the American traditions my mother clings to religiously. I talked to my parents yesterday. They're disappointed that we won't be home for Thanksgiving, but my mother assured me that we would have a wonderful Christmas together."

Tamra made a pleasurable noise. "That sounds nice. We're getting in on all kinds of celebrations, aren't we?"

"We certainly are," Jess said. "And soon after New Year's, we'll be celebrating our marriage."

Tamra shot him a startled glance, then wished she'd been more careful when his brow furrowed. She closed her eyes to avoid his gaze, but the weight of his sigh was evident. "You know," he said, "I'm getting tired of having you respond that way whenever marrying me comes up." He paused and added, "Do you want to marry me, Tamra?"

"Of course," she said without looking at him.

"Then . . . what's wrong?" When she said nothing, he pressed. "Talk to me . . . please?"

"There's nothing to say that hasn't been said before." She squeezed his hand and opened her eyes. "Don't worry, Jess. It's just that . . . a lot has happened and I just need to let it all catch up with me." She reached up and touched his face. "I love you. I *need* you."

Jess nodded but he didn't look convinced. He pressed a kiss to her brow and came to his feet. "I bet you're starved. I'll dig you up something to eat."

He said nothing more as he brought her a tray with chicken noodle soup, saltine crackers, and apple juice. But Tamra sensed the tension between them. She wanted to alleviate it, but she didn't know what to say. She could hardly explain to him why she felt these subtle nagging doubts, when she didn't understand it herself.

Food tasted good to her for the first time since she'd become ill, and she asked for a second helping. With her stomach full, Tamra slept until Jess woke her with a dinner tray. Again she ate heartily. Emma and Allison both checked in on her, thrilled to know she was on the mend. She slept again until morning and woke to find she felt considerably better, but through the day she found a familiar uneasiness nagging at her. She knew she'd brought it with her from Minneapolis, but being ill had made it easy to ignore her emotions. Through the course of the day Jess asked her several times if she was all right, if she needed to talk. She insisted she was fine but felt certain he saw through her.

After Tamra ate supper at the table with the family, she laid down on the couch in the family room, sick to death of the room she'd hardly left for a week and a half. She felt guilty listening to the work of cleaning up the kitchen, wishing she felt well enough to help. Jess sat down across from her and put his bare feet up on the coffee table.

"Oh, by the way," he said, "Sean's coming by."

"Is he bringing the family?" she asked, wondering when she'd get a chance to meet them.

"No," Jess drawled with something cautious in his eyes.

Tamra lifted her head to look at him pointedly. Recalling that Sean was a psychologist, she asked tersely, *"Why* is Sean coming over?"

"To talk," he said without apology. He lightly added, "It's great to have a shrink in the family, especially for people like me with suicidal tendencies."

"Are you having suicidal tendencies?" Tamra asked.

"No. Are you?" he countered, a little too seriously. When she didn't answer he added, "You don't have to sit up, but you *do* have to talk."

"About what?" she demanded.

"That's what I'd like to know," he said. "If I could get you to talk, I wouldn't have to arrange premarital counseling."

Tamra scowled at him, trying to think of any excuse to be angry with Jess and leave the room. But his expression showed concern and his voice was gentle as he leaned forward and said, "Listen to me, Tamra. I'm not trying to put you on the spot or cause problems here. But Sean just has a way of making sense of things that I have trouble making sense of. And maybe if we could just . . . talk to him, we could—"

"What did you tell him?" she asked, wishing it hadn't sounded so harsh.

Jess answered evenly. "I told him you had a rough upbringing and you'd had some difficult encounters with your mother recently, and I was under the impression it was bothering you a lot more than you were letting on."

While Tamra wanted to tell Jess he was out of line and making something out of nothing, an unexpected surge of tears leaked out with no warning. She pressed a hand over her eyes as she heard Allison enter the room, saying, "Okay, we're off. Have a good time."

"Where are you going?" Tamra asked, looking up at her now that she'd managed to fight the tears back.

"Oh, we're all going to the movies," she said brightly and Jess smirked.

When the entire family had left, including Emma, Tamra said to Jess, "Looks like you've got this all very cleverly arranged."

Before he could respond, the doorbell rang. "Yeah, I do," he bragged and came to his feet. "That would be the shrink. Try to be civil."

Tamra forced herself to breathe deeply and not be angry while Jess went to answer the door. She knew he was only concerned and trying to look out for her best interests. Perhaps Sean *could* help her make sense of what she was feeling.

"Hey there," Sean O'Hara said, walking into the room at Jess's side. "I understand you've been pretty sick."

"Yeah, but I'm feeling a lot better now," Tamra said. "How are you?"

"Oh, I'm great," Sean said, sitting across the room as if he'd been in this house hundreds of times. Jess had said that Sean was practically like a brother, and she felt certain that he kept a close relationship with Jess's siblings who lived here in the same city.

While Tamra expected some uncomfortable small talk, Sean quickly went on to say, "So, I understand you've had some rough things come up lately."

"Yes, well . . . I suppose I have, but . . . I must admit I'm really not in the mood to talk about it."

Sean shrugged his shoulders. "That's okay. But you might be interested to know that from what Jess tells me, I think we might have a great deal in common."

"Really?" Tamra said, surprised by his approach.

"Well, for one thing," Sean said, "when I joined the Church, I was completely cut off by my family. My father threw me out and threatened every other family member with the same if they associated with me at all."

"Good heavens," Tamra muttered breathlessly, feeling her heart quicken. She vaguely recalled now that Jess had once mentioned something of Sean's situation, but she'd completely forgotten. She was surprised at how it validated her feelings to personally know someone else who knew how she might feel. And it comforted her just to know that someone so confident and apparently happy had been through something so difficult. As Sean went on to briefly explain the circumstances behind his joining the Church and the ensuing struggles, her heart went out to him and she felt warmed by the growing bond they shared. He told her how he had eventually bridged the gap with his parents, but only after some extremely difficult encounters. He talked about the things he'd learned through his trials, about faith, about the Atonement, and about breaking dysfunctional cycles in order to make life better for the next generation than it was for them.

Sean spoke of his rebellious youth and some bad choices he'd made that had brought a great deal of grief into his life, and how important it was to put the past in the past, whether the misery found there was of your own doing or someone else's. Jess piped in with similar feelings, talking of how the bad choices he'd made in his youth made him feel unworthy of being blessed, or feeling the Spirit. Because he'd never fully forgiven himself or accepted the Atonement on behalf of the sins he'd committed, he felt that somehow he'd been responsible for the accident—that he was to blame.

While Tamra watched Jess and Sean converse almost as if she weren't there, each getting a little emotional here and there, she marveled at the warm spirit hovering in the room, and the comfort she felt from all she was hearing and feeling. When the conversation finally came around to easy bantering about memories the two men shared from many years ago, Tamra realized their little *counseling session* had come to an end—and she'd hardly said a word.

As Sean rose to leave, he said directly to Tamra, "You're an amazing woman, Tamra, and you're going to be just fine."

"How do you know that?" she asked.

"Well," he chuckled, "practically every member of the family has raved about your fine qualities, and . . . well, it's not difficult to see that they're right. Jess is a very lucky man."

Tamra smiled up at Jess and admitted, "I believe I'm the lucky one. Thank you," she said, turning again to Sean.

"All I did was ramble and reminisce a bit." Sean chuckled humbly.

"Well, it helped," Tamra said, "so thanks anyway."

"You're welcome. Call me any time if you need to talk." He turned to Jess. "Either one of you." He lightly slapped Jess's shoulder. "After all, we're family."

"So we are," Jess said and walked Sean to the door. Overhearing their exchange, Tamra realized that Sean and his family were headed out of town for the holiday, and they wouldn't see him again before they left for Australia. Tamra felt disappointed to realize she would have to wait to meet his wife and children, but she concluded that it gave her something to look forward to.

Jess returned after Sean had left and sat beside Tamra. "Are you still mad at me?"

"I wasn't mad at you," she insisted. He looked skeptical and she added, "Just . . . frustrated."

"Okay. Are you still *frustrated?*"

"No. I believe I feel a little better actually." She sighed loudly. "I'm not sure I fully understand what's really troubling me; maybe it's just . . . habit, or something. But I do feel better." She smiled at Jess and touched his face. "Just be patient with me."

He smiled in return. "Darlin', in the patience department, I am forever indebted—and forever is how long I've got."

He kissed her, then spoke close to her face. "It's nice to kiss you again, now that you're rid of those nasty germs."

"Amen," she said and kissed him again.

* * *

A subtle warmth hovered with Tamra as she celebrated Thanksgiving with Jess at her side. She didn't have much strength for working in the kitchen, but the spirit of their celebration encircled her as she stayed in the middle of the preparations, helping a little here and there. Several times through the day, Tamra felt close to tears, filled with gratitude for the opportunity she'd been blessed with to become a part of Jess's life—and his family. She had certainly enjoyed and appreciated the celebration they'd shared with her father and stepmother, but there was a spirit in Ammon and Allison's home that hadn't been present there. Simply put, this family had the gospel. And for that alone, Tamra felt deeply grateful.

Snow began falling late in the afternoon, and it continued all through the night. Tamra wasn't terribly surprised when Jess sneaked into her room and woke her just past dawn, without disturbing

Emma. "Hey," he whispered, "do you think you feel good enough to help me build a snowman?"

Tamra chuckled quietly. "I think I could manage, as long as I can take a nap afterward."

"Deal," he said, and he left her to get dressed. Emma rolled over and gave her an inquisitive gaze, then drifted back to sleep before Tamra slipped quietly from the room to find Jess waiting in the hall. She finished putting on her winter clothing in the family room, then they crept out the front door. Jess laughed and said, "Now, *this* is snow."

Tamra soon realized what he meant when Jess began making snowballs and throwing them at her. She caught on quickly and began retaliating while they laughed together, trying not to be too loud and wake the family—if not the neighbors. The snow was wet and perfect for packing tightly, and they worked together to make a large snowman. She laughed when Jess pulled from his pockets some cookies and red licorice that he used to make buttons and a face. And he pulled from inside his coat a hat he'd made from a paper sack.

"You came prepared," she said.

"Yes, I did." He laughed and planted it firmly on the snowman's head, making certain it wouldn't blow away.

"Now," he said, "everyone who goes down this street will have to pass by Parson Brown, and he will make them all smile."

"Parson Brown?" she asked.

"You know . . . in the song."

"It sounds familiar, but I'm not placing it," she said.

Jess began to sing, *"In the meadow we can build a snowman, and pretend that he is Parson Brown. He'll say are you married? We'll say, 'No, man. But you can do the job while you're in town.'"*

"Oh, *that* song," Tamra said. "Well, you know what, if that snowman marries us, it won't be forever."

"That's true," Jess said, wishing he could tell her how good it felt to hear her speak positively of their plans to marry. "But I can assure you that whoever *does* marry us will be wearing the same color."

Tamra laughed. "So he will." She then sang to him, *"Later on we'll conspire, as we dream by the fire, to face unafraid the plans that we made, walking in a winter wonderland."*

Their eyes met, and a look filled with volumes of the hopes and dreams passed silently between them. Jess felt his heart leap with joy that the difficulties had not totally marred her belief in their future.

Jess and Tamra were sitting at the kitchen table, sipping from cups of hot chocolate, when Allison appeared, tying a bathrobe around her waist.

"Well, good morning," she said. "What are the two of you up to?"

"Just recovering," Jess said with a smirk and a wink.

"Recovering?" Allison echoed, pouring herself a cup of hot water from the teapot on the stove.

"Yes," Tamra said, "we were up early making Parson Brown there on the front lawn."

Allison chuckled and took a long gaze out the window then grinned. "How quaint," she said.

"You can't make a snowman in Minneapolis," he said gravely. "Dreadful place."

"You can't make a snowman at home, either," Allison pointed out.

"Yes, but," Jess lifted an authoritative finger, "one would not *expect* to make a snowman where it doesn't snow. When you get lots of snow and you can't do anything fun with it, now that's a crime." He smirked again at Tamra. "I don't know how you could ever recover from such dreadful conditions in your youth." He shook his head and clucked his tongue. "No snowmen; no snowball fights."

Jess felt his peace deepen when she smiled and said, "I'm counting on you to make up for my . . . *dreadful youth.*"

"It would be a pleasure," Jess said.

While Allison stirred her hot chocolate, she said, "I hope you don't have any big plans today, because it just might be the perfect day to do something we only get to do once or twice every winter; the conditions have to be just right."

"What?" Jess asked like a child.

"Did you ever go with us to Ammon's grandmother's home in Spanish Fork?"

"I believe so," Jess said. "But hasn't his grandmother passed away?"

"She has, but his sister, Sariah, lives in the home with her family." Allison smiled and added, "Did you ever go sleigh riding with us?"

Jess lifted his brows and drawled, "No." His tone of voice implied that she'd been keeping secrets from him and he wasn't very happy about it.

"Well, it was a tradition in Ammon's family," Allison explained. "Of course, these days the roads get scraped and the snow melts off quickly. But there are still some back roads that will work on a day like today with all this fresh snow . . . if you're game."

"Game?" Jess echoed. "Good heavens; it sounds divine. When do we leave?"

"Just as soon as everyone gets up and eats breakfast."

Jess rose to his feet. "I'll wake the little beasts. You ladies slap some pancakes on the stove, or something."

Tamra laughed as Allison grabbed his arm and said, "No, I'll wake the little beasts *and* the big beasts. *You* slap some pancakes together."

"Can you do animal pancakes like your father?" Tamra asked him.

"Not really. I don't have the finesse."

"Well, you could use some practice then," Allison said and left the room.

After everyone had eaten breakfast, they drove in two vehicles to Spanish Fork. Tamra was glad to be riding with Allison as she described the Christmas she had spent with Ammon's family at his grandmother's home, when he had proposed to her in front of the entire family. When they arrived at the house, the children all ran in to greet their cousins. Tamra enjoyed meeting Sariah and her family. Ammon's sister had similar coloring and was equally attractive. Tamra couldn't keep track of her children's names, especially when she hadn't even mastered the names of Allison's children yet, and they would soon be her nieces and nephews.

Jess laughed and Tamra squealed aloud when she saw the old but well-kept sleigh. Jess helped Ammon harness the horses, then they piled in and snuggled beneath quilts thrown over their laps. With the snow glistening in the sun, and the sleigh runners gliding gently over the endless sea of white, Tamra snuggled close to Jess and just soaked in the magic aura surrounding her. At such moments, she could almost believe that it was possible to put her ugly past behind once and for all.

The remainder of the day was equally enjoyable as they all went to a matinee movie, then home to play board games until late. Lying in bed that night, Tamra pondered all she had experienced since she'd left

Australia, then she considered the feelings that had led her to become involved with the Hamilton family in the first place. She truly was blessed; if only she could feel completely worthy of such blessings. If only she could put the past behind her, completely and for good.

Saturday morning, Jess and Tamra drove to the heart of Salt Lake City. Jess parked the car in the underground garage of one of the downtown malls, and they walked hand in hand through the mall and across the street to the Joseph Smith Memorial building. They saw an incredible film there, then went to the top floor to look west toward Temple Square. After sharing lunch, they went into the temple and went through an endowment session.

Tamra felt the Spirit close, especially at a particular point when she looked at Jess across the room and was overcome with a sensation not unlike what she'd felt the first time she had looked at him. She considered the possibility that they had truly loved each other in the life before this one, and the warmth inside of her deepened. She pondered the conversations they'd had with Sean O'Hara a few days earlier. And while a subtle uneasiness remained within her, she knew in her heart that pressing forward on this path with Jess was the right thing to do with her life. She simply had to have the faith that everything else would work itself out.

They sat close together in the celestial room, holding hands, for nearly an hour. Jess spoke reverently of the experiences that had transformed his heart and soul. Tamra shared her own conversion experience with him in a way she never had before, and they found the similarities amazing. They concluded that whether you were raised in the Church or joined as an adult, there came a time when personal conversion was a necessary step on the road to eternal salvation.

Tamra was hungry again by the time they had changed back into their street clothes, so they ate supper in the temple cafeteria. When they walked outside to find it dark, Tamra became immediately fascinated by the incredible beauty of Temple Square and the Main Street Plaza, especially at this time of year, filled with Christmas lights and decor. They wandered about, holding hands, for most of the evening, going intermittently into the visitors centers in order to warm up. She marveled at the beauty of the temple itself, with its spires lit up brilliantly. But pondering all she had felt within its walls, she knew that she preferred to be inside. Their excursion was made complete with a carriage ride through the heart of the city.

"Oh, I love it here," Tamra said, resting her head on Jess's shoulder. "We must come back to Salt Lake City."

"With relatives less than an hour away, that shouldn't be a problem," he said.

That night Tamra dreamt that she was back in Australia, sitting on the veranda of the house where they would live, along with Jess's parents. She woke up missing the place that had quickly become her home, and was relieved to realize they would be leaving the next day. They planned to stop in California to see another of Jess's sisters, but they would only be staying one night.

It was difficult to say good-bye to Emma and Allison and all of Allison's family, but they would be coming to Australia for the wedding, so it wouldn't be very many weeks before they saw each other again. On the plane, Tamra was struck by how few weeks they really had until the wedding, but her excitement was mingled with that ever-present, underlying uneasiness. She wished she knew how to make it go away so she could just enjoy every moment of her life.

They were met at the Sacramento airport by Jess's sister, Alexa. Tamra almost envied her having such a name, knowing that she was named after Jess's great-great-grandmother, a woman that Tamra admired deeply for many reasons. Tamra had met Alexa when she'd come to Australia several months ago and, just as with his other sisters, she looked forward to getting to know her better.

The drive to Alexa's home took nearly an hour, but Tamra enjoyed their visit. When they arrived, she was amazed at how much Bridger had grown since he'd come to Australia with his mother. Bridger wasn't much older than Evelyn, and being with him made Tamra miss her immensely. Jess admitted to feeling the same way, and they were both glad to know they would soon be seeing her again. They couldn't talk about Evelyn without speculating over how it would be when they were able to officially adopt her. The passing of time had only made both of them more fully convinced that it was the right thing to do. For Tamra, it seemed the most natural thing in the world to raise this child as her own.

Tamra enjoyed meeting Alexa's husband, Dale, and their other four children, including a set of twins who were now nine. The children stayed at home that evening while the adults went out to dinner. Tamra enjoyed the evening, but felt especially tired when they returned home. She reasoned that her recent illness combined with busy days and travel was wearing on her. She slept deeply and woke late to find Jess and Alexa visiting in the front room. Dale had gone to work, and the children to school, except for Bridger, who was playing with puzzles on the floor. Tamra visited with them for a few minutes, then excused herself to take a shower. She was barely dressed when Jess knocked at her bedroom door.

"Come in," she called.

He stepped inside and handed her the cordless phone, saying, "It's for you."

She asked in a whisper, "Who is it?"

"It's my father," Jess said. "He wants to talk to you."

Tamra felt her heart quicken as she took the phone. She knew that Jess talked with his parents every few days, and he was often relaying their conversations. But she hadn't actually talked to Jess's father since the day she'd flown out of Australia.

"Hello?" she said.

"Hi there, sweetie," Michael said, and Tamara suddenly realized how much she had missed him.

"Hello," she repeated, more eagerly.

"I hope you're not going to find any more excuses to keep from coming home. We miss you."

"Well, I miss you too," she said. "And barring any more unexpected illnesses, we should be on our way out of the country this evening."

"Good. We're counting the hours," he said.

Following a moment of silence, she asked, "Was that why you wanted to talk to me? To tell me that you miss me?"

"Partly," he said.

"And the other part would be . . . what? I mean, don't get me wrong. It's good to talk to you, but I'm just . . . wondering."

"The thing is," Michael's voice softened, "Jess has told us a little of what you've been struggling with. I hope you don't mind. You've been like family since the day you came to our home and . . ."

"I don't mind," she said. "After what we went through with Jess, we pretty well established being open about our problems."

"Yes, that's true," Michael said. "You've been on my mind quite a bit lately, and there was something about my grandfather's experiences that kept lingering in my mind. I went back to read a few pieces in his journals, with you in mind, and there's a point that I thought might help."

"Okay," she said, wondering what insight she might have missed. "You know, of course, that I've read all of the journals."

"Yes, I know, but . . . there's something that's not recorded in his journals—something I heard him say."

Tamra was momentarily taken aback. She had come to know the first Michael Hamilton fairly well through his journals, and the journals of his family members. Her mental images of him were surrounded by history and adventure. He had barely been an adult at the dawn of the twentieth century. She knew he was Michael's grandfather and namesake, but it had simply never occurred to her that Michael had actually conversed and interacted with this man that Tamra considered practically a legend.

"Are you okay?" Michael asked, startling her from her thoughts.

"Yes, of course. Just . . . surprised. I simply hadn't considered that you would have known him when he was living."

Michael chuckled. "Knowing him was one of the greatest privileges of my childhood. My memories of him are very clear—likely because he was such an impressive man. Of course, I remember him as strong and confident, self-assured and compassionate. But you know from his journals that he had a terribly troubled childhood."

"Horrific, more like," Tamra said, recalling different tidbits from the family journals. Alexandra Byrnehouse-Davies had nurtured Michael as a boy in the boys' home, and he had much later married Alexa's daughter, Emma. Alexa and Emma had both written of their heartache in learning about Michael's childhood abuse—abuse that had spurred him to a life on the streets at a very young age. While there had been no details in the journal, she recalled phrases like *severe abuse, ghastly scars,* and *too horrible to imagine.*

"Yes, horrific would be accurate, I believe," Michael said. "But you know, he didn't say much in his journals about his life before coming here. And as a child, I had no idea what his upbringing had entailed beyond him frequently joking about being taken in by the family as a lost soul. But I firmly remember a conversation he had with my mother at a time when she was upset over something—I have no idea what. He told her that the most profound lesson he had learned in his life was that he would never be able to find his value as a person through the eyes of those who had treated him badly. He had come to understand that their problems had nothing to do with him, that they were only perpetuating pain from their own difficult experiences, and judging them or holding onto what they had done would only bring more grief upon himself. He said that God had sent people into his life who loved him, and that was enough for him to know that he was redeemable."

Tamra felt Michael's words penetrate to the deepest part of her, filling her with a warmth that seemed to verify the truth of his grandfather's words. He was silent a moment then he chuckled softly. "I'm amazed at how clearly I've remembered those words, when so many memories of my childhood have completely faded."

"Perhaps you *needed* to remember," Tamra said, hearing her voice break.

"Yes, I believe I did. I was touched by his words at the time, even though I was a young child and I had no idea how profound they were. It was many years, long after he'd died, before I read the journals and fully understood the implication of what he'd been talking about. And I remember weeping when it struck me. He had been through far more than most human beings could ever endure, but he rose above it and broke the cycle to become one of the finest men I have ever known. I've often thought that one of the great legacies of this family is the breaking of those dysfunctional cycles."

Again there was silence. Tamra could hardly find her voice amidst the emotion that had overcome her. Michael finally went on. "If you don't mind, I'd like to add some of my own personal wisdom; something else that's been on my mind as I've thought of what you're struggling with."

Tamra cleared her throat. "Of course," she said, her voice barely steady. "I'd love to hear it."

"I believe you know there was a time in my life when I was struggling deeply with some fears and emotions that got the better of me. It was all tied into that accident when Emily . . . nearly died."

Tamra heard the tightness in his voice, just as she had the last time it had come up in a family discussion following Jess's suicide attempt. Tamra knew very little beyond it being a traumatic experience for the entire family, and apparently Michael had been angry while he was driving, which had been the reason for the accident. Michael's regret was as evident now as it had been then.

"I'm not going to bore you with the details, Tamra," he went on. "The important thing is this: the one thing that kept me from coming to terms with all that was bothering me . . . The one thing I had overlooked was simply . . . forgiveness. I hadn't consciously harbored ill feelings, but when I really started soul searching, I realized they were there—cankering my soul. When I truly forgave those who had brought pain into my life—and Emily's—including myself, I was able to get beyond the problem and find peace. That was the key for me, Tamra. It was forgiveness. I'm not saying that's the case with you. I'm only telling you that I felt compelled to share that with you. Maybe it will at least give you something to think about."

Tamra wiped at the tears on her face and forced herself to speak, even though her emotions were readily evident. "Yes, actually . . . I think it gives me a great deal to think about. Thank you."

"Remember, Tamra, the price has already been paid for your burdens. You don't have to carry them, and your Savior doesn't want you to."

Tamra cried for ten minutes after she hung up the phone, feeling Michael's love and concern still wrapped securely around her. As the memory of his words continued to parade around in her mind, she instinctively knew that she had found the final pieces to the puzzle; she only had to find a way to make them fit.

Chapter Nine

Tamra pulled herself together and went to the kitchen to find that it was nearly time for lunch, so she skipped breakfast and made herself a sandwich. Jess and Alexa soon joined her, but neither of them asked about her conversation with their father, even though she sensed they were both curious.

After visiting a while longer, Jess and Tamra had to pack their bags, and Alexa drove them back to the airport. Saying good-bye, Tamra was once again grateful to know that they would all be together for the wedding. She had truly grown to love Jess's family—all of them.

They caught a short flight that would take them to L.A., where they would connect with an overseas flight. It wasn't until they were in the air that Jess asked in a soft voice, "So, what did my father have to say?"

Tamra was surprised at how quickly her emotions surfaced again. She shook her head briefly and looked away. He took her hand, saying, "He didn't hurt your feelings, did he? Because if he did, I'm going to have to give him a piece of my mind when we get home."

"No," she chuckled through her tears, "he didn't hurt my feelings. In truth . . . I think he was inspired to say what he did, and given some time to think about it, I believe I just might have the answer."

"What did he say?" Jess asked when she hesitated too long.

Tamra sighed deeply. "He talked about his grandfather . . . and himself. He told me that when he was going through a difficult time in his life, he finally realized that the one thing he'd overlooked was forgiveness. When he'd been able to forgive someone he'd held ill feelings toward, he was able to come to terms with what had been troubling him."

Jess thought about it for a minute before he said, "Oh, I see. And so . . . are you thinking that the problem is in holding ill feelings toward your mother?"

Tamra nodded, too emotional to speak. Jess put his arm around her and let her cry silently against his shoulder. When she regained her composure, she admitted, "But . . . while I was packing . . . I got down on my knees . . . and I asked the Lord to help me forgive my mother and put it behind me and . . ." The tears came again, but they were cleansing tears, and she relished them. "I was amazed, Jess," she said, looking into his eyes, "how quickly peace came over me, and I knew that I *had* forgiven her. I simply had to ask the Lord to take the burden from me, and He did. As soon as I asked, He did. Of course, I think it's something I've been working at for many years, so I can't say it just magically happened in an instant. It's more like . . . this was the final step to make my forgiveness complete."

Jess felt overcome with emotion as he looked into her eyes and knew exactly how she felt. He was unable to speak, but embracing her tightly, he felt certain that she knew how deeply grateful he was for all they had been blessed with, most especially the gospel that enriched their lives and made their struggles bearable.

"And something else occurred to me," she said after blowing her nose. "I was in the temple in Sydney when I made the decision to come to the States and see my mother. So much has happened—and it's been such an emotional roller coaster—that I lost sight of what I'd felt when I made that decision."

"And what was that?" he asked when she hesitated.

"It was the spirit of Elijah," she said in little more than a whisper. "I realized that I had put countless hours into doing genealogy and temple work, but I needed to consider my family members who were still *living*. Of course, at the time, I had no intention of trying to find my father, and I had no idea that I had a living grandmother. But now . . . it all makes so much sense. And even though it's been rough, I'm just . . . grateful for all that's happened."

"So am I," Jess said as he took her hand and kissed it.

Through the remainder of the flight, Tamra pondered all she'd felt this day and was comforted by the wondrous, cleansing feeling of forgiveness. She concluded that while it was still difficult to accept her mother's bad attitude toward her, she had been able to finally fully let go of the difficulties of her childhood. She was grateful for some time in the L.A. airport. At a gift shop she bought a beautiful Christmas card, and after they'd gotten something to eat, she pulled it out and wrote some careful words to her mother. She told her that, in spite of their differences, it had been good to see her, and that she hoped they would be able to keep in touch. She struggled for just the right words to say what she *really* needed to say. She closed her eyes and prayed for guidance, knowing her time was brief, and she wanted to mail the card before they left the country. Finally she was able to write: *We both know that my childhood was difficult for many reasons, and I must confess that I have struggled with my feelings concerning much of what happened. I must also admit that I've harbored difficult feelings toward you for many years, in spite of the changes I've made in my life. I don't know if it will mean anything to you, but it means a great deal to me to let you know that I no longer hold any ill feelings. I have forgiven you for all that happened, whether you might have been directly responsible or not. I'm putting the past behind me from this moment, and I'm hoping you will be able to do the same. May this Christmas season be bright for you. I hope we'll be able to see each other again before long. Love, your daughter, Tamra.*

Tamra read it through, then had Jess do the same. When he told her it sounded fine, she took a deep breath, sealed it up, and dropped it into a mailbox before she had too much time to think about it. In spite of herself, she couldn't help wondering if her mother would scoff at her words and throw the card away. Unable to bear such a thought, she forced the possibility out of her mind and reminded herself that she had done the right thing. She had done all she could do; her mother's free agency was something she had no control over.

When the plane rose into the night sky and they finally left the country, Tamra felt a deep peace settle over her. The miracle of forgiveness left her in awe, and she felt certain that the spirit of Elijah had been a part of the miracle. She had done all she could to turn her heart to those who had gone before her, both living and dead. Now she could only pray that the miracle might go full circle, and that her mother's heart would be softened toward her.

With Jess's hand in hers, she contemplated all that had happened since they had arrived together in the States a few weeks ago. With his love and guidance, she had built many bridges and strengthened other, weaker ones. She drifted to sleep with warm memories of days spent with her father and stepmother and grandmother, and members of Jess's family. She awoke to daylight seeping through the cabin windows, feeling a bright hope of returning to the home she had grown to love so dearly, to Jess's parents who had loved and accepted her fully, and to little Evelyn, who had no comprehension of the changes that would soon occur in her life, but only in technicality. She would still live in the same home and be surrounded by the same people who loved her.

Tamra smiled at the vision in her mind of how their life together would be. Jess kissed her cheek and laughed softly, close to her ear, as if he could sense her thoughts.

"I love you, Tamra," he said, gazing into her eyes.

"And I love you," she replied and touched his face. She simply couldn't imagine that life might get any better than this, and yet their life together was only beginning.

* * *

Jess had once thought that they would stop to see Tamra's Aunt Rhea in Sydney, and his sister, Amee, and her family in Adelaide. But they were both terribly anxious to get home and opted for phone calls from Sydney before they embarked on the final leg of their journey.

"Hey, I just thought of something," Tamra said, hesitating to dial her aunt's number.

"What?" Jess asked, leaning against the phone booth.

"How are we getting home from here?"

He smiled and asked, "Why?"

"Because we can't drive two cars to Queensland; well, I guess we *could,* but it would be awfully tedious not to be in the same vehicle with you, and—"

"We're flying," he said.

Tamra smiled, recalling that his family owned private planes; she'd honestly forgotten. "Okay," she said, "but when your sisters came, your dad picked them up, and you didn't tell him to—"

"I can fly the thing," he said smugly. "How do you think I got here?"

"Oh, I see." She smiled more widely. "Well, this ought to be an adventure."

"So, you trust me to fly you safely home?"

Tamra caught the undertone in his words. She knew well how difficult it had been for him to drive a vehicle again following the accident. Surely flying a plane would fall under the same category. But it was easy for Tamra to say, "I've told you before, my patriarchal blessing says that I'm going to live a full life with many children and grandchildren. If I feel inspired to not get in a car—or a plane—with you, I'll let you know."

He chuckled and she added, "My car is at my aunt's house. I left it at a hotel near the airport and had her pick it up. If I'm flying home, then . . ."

"Just ask her if it's in the way. If it's not, tell her to use it if she needs it and . . . we'll figure something out later."

Tamra nodded and dialed her aunt's number. They talked and laughed for several minutes, then Jess got on the phone and they too had a great deal to say. Much had happened since he had last seen Rhea, when she had helped him learn that Tamra was flying to the States. Tamra was grateful that Jess genuinely liked the woman, and that he looked forward to getting to know her better. She knew he found Rhea's warmth and positive attitude a stark contrast to Tamra's mother, who had been the cause of so much grief through Tamra's life—including the past few weeks.

Rhea said keeping the car wouldn't be a problem, and if nothing else came up, she'd just drive it to the wedding reception that would be held at their home in Queensland next month.

Jess called his sister and they both talked with her for a few minutes, then they got something to eat and were soon flying toward home, with Jess calmly in control of the plane.

"This is nice," Tamra said, gazing out the window at the incredible view of the countryside below.

"Yes, it is," he said, reaching for her hand.

Tamra drifted to sleep until Jess nudged her and said, "We're there, darlin'." She smiled and stretched. She loved it when he called her that; she'd heard his father call his mother that many times, with deep affection.

Gazing out the window, Tamra felt goose bumps all over her. "It's even more beautiful from the air," she said, noting the house surrounded by trees, the stables, the race track, and the boys' home that had become so close to her heart. Warmth overtook her again to see the gables jutting out from the upper floor of the boys' home. She could never forget how she'd felt the first time she'd seen them, as if her spirit had sensed that they had deep significance in her life, even though she'd had no idea what that significance was at the time.

Jess circled the plane low near the house, which Tamra knew was customary from the times that Michael had flown in. This let everyone know they'd arrived, and someone would drive out to the hangar and meet them. Tamra laughed to see Michael step down from the veranda and wave to them. She had missed him so much! He had been the father she'd never had. And even now that she'd found her father and bridged the gap between them, there was something about the way Michael Hamilton treated her that made her feel her worth. She recalled his recent phone call, and the words that had been so inspired, and she felt deeply grateful to be part of such a family.

Tamra laughed again when Emily appeared on the lawn as well, waving jubilantly. Emily too had been a profound source of wisdom, love, and acceptance. Just seeing her again made Tamra realize that living in the same home with Emily Hamilton could more than compensate for all that was lacking in the relationship with her own mother.

Jess flew the plane to a long stretch of flat land that had been cleared for a runway. He brought the plane down smoothly and pulled it into the hangar just as a Toyota Land Cruiser appeared with a cloud of dust trailing behind it. Jess had barely helped Tamra out of the plane before she was embraced heartily, first by Emily, and then by Michael. Jess was greeted with equal exuberance before the hangar was locked up and their luggage was put into the Cruiser.

The short drive to the house was filled with questions about their trip, although there wasn't much they didn't already know from frequent phone calls. Tamra felt distracted from the conversation as they passed by the boys' home and the gables came into view. She found them somehow symbolic of the great legacy of this family, and just seeing them made her wonder how she ever could have doubted her place with these people. She had felt it deeply from the first day she'd come here. And now, with Jess's hand in hers, and their wedding only weeks away, she knew in her heart that this place was meant to be her home for as long as she remained on this earth.

The minute they stepped inside the house, Jess expressed Tamra's thoughts perfectly when he asked, "Where is Evelyn?"

"I believe she's up in the nursery with Sadie," Emily said. "You take your luggage up and go see her; we'll finish getting supper on."

"It's sure good to have you home," Michael said, smiling at Tamra and Jess.

"And it's good to be home," Jess said. "And together," he added, taking Tamra's hand.

"Amen," Emily and Tamra both said at the same time, then laughed.

Tamra followed Jess up the stairs while he carried the majority of the luggage, as he always did. But he left it on the landing and went directly to the nursery. Approaching the open door, Tamra could hear Sadie's familiar voice, reading a story aloud. Sadie was more like family than an employee. She took great joy in helping around the house and spending time with little Evelyn.

Jess and Tamra both hesitated in the doorway to take in the tender scene. Sadie looked just the same; she was a slightly thick, rumpled woman in her late fifties. Her gray hair was cut short and full of tight curls that clung close to her head. She wore thick-rimmed glasses that framed her smiling eyes. But Tamra's attention was drawn more to Evelyn just as Jess squeezed her hand tightly, letting her know that he shared her thoughts. They had both felt strongly that adopting Evelyn to raise as their own was the right thing to do. But Tamra hadn't seen the child since the decision had been reached, and now her eyes filled with warm tears that seemed to confirm the rightness of being Evelyn's mother on this earth.

Evelyn seemed to have changed since Tamra had last seen her. Her reddish-blonde hair had grown a bit and hung almost to her shoulders. But her smile was still as bright when she caught movement near the door and looked in their direction. "Mama, Daddy!" she squealed and jumped down from Sadie's lap to run toward them. Tamra's emotions heightened at this response. She had forgotten that Evelyn had often called her "Mama," as she did many women; since her own mother had died in her infancy, she seemed to connect the word with a grown woman. For the same reason, she had often called Jess "Daddy." But prior to today, Tamra had seen him show very little interest in the child, as if her presence had only been a painful reminder of the deaths of his brother and sister-in-law.

Now Evelyn rushed toward Jess and he scooped her into his arms, laughing heartily. Tamra looked on in awe. She could almost sense how Evelyn's tender spirit had known long before either of them had that they were meant to be a family. Could that be why Evelyn had been more consistent in referring to them as "Mama and Daddy" than she had other people? A bizarre likelihood perhaps, but given the spiritual nature of life, Tamra couldn't deny that it was possible.

Jess took Evelyn with him to his room to unpack, and Tamra couldn't resist tagging along. Then they all went to Tamra's room and did the same, laughing every few minutes over Evelyn's childish antics.

Gathering in the kitchen for supper felt warm and familiar to Tamra. There was only one real difference, and that was the peace and happiness she saw in Jess's eyes. She truly had come home.

Everyone lingered at the table long after the meal was over, chatting and laughing as they caught up on the weeks since they'd been together, and discussing wedding plans. While Evelyn played in the next room, Tamra felt Jess's hand slip into hers. Everything combined together to make her realize that they would actually soon be married.

When Sadie announced that she was taking Evelyn upstairs to bathe her and put her to bed, Jess rose to his feet and said, "No, it's my turn." In response to their startled glances, he just smiled and added, "But Tamra's going to help me."

While Evelyn sat in the tub, lining up a number of floating toys, Tamra kissed Jess quickly and muttered, "I love you, Jess Hamilton."

He kissed her again. "I love you too, Tamra Hamilton-almost."

When Evelyn was finally in bed, Jess admitted, "I'm exhausted, but not terribly sleepy. How about a few minutes on the veranda?"

"Sounds delightful." Tamra slipped her hand into his and they walked downstairs and outside.

A partial moon, surrounded by stars scattered beyond the perimeter of its glow, illuminated the yard as they stood together to take in the view. Tamra touched the little silver star hanging on a chain around her neck. She recalled fondly the day her father and Claudia had given it to her, and Claudia's brief explanation. *When I saw it, I thought of what you'd said about the star on the Christmas tree. So the necklace is to remind you that no matter how far apart we are, you have family that love you, and we'll always be here to help get you through whatever life might dish out.*

Tamra's mind went back a little further, recalling well the words she'd said to Claudia that had apparently inspired the purchase. *A star is such a wonderful symbol . . . It's something that gives light and guides you through the darkness.*

Tamra sighed and absorbed the star-lit sky once more. She certainly had been given a great deal of light that had guided her through much darkness, and now she had her whole life ahead of her, with the love of many good people, and the light of the gospel to continue guiding her through whatever might lie ahead.

Following a few minutes of silence, Tamra admitted almost dreamily, "I'm so happy, Jess."

"Are you really?" he asked, turning to lean back against the veranda rail.

"Oh, I am." She looked up at the moon. "I know life will bring challenges, but to be able to face them together . . . and to live here in this beautiful place, with so many good people who love us, and with the gospel in our lives . . . how could I ask for more than that?"

"I certainly couldn't," he said firmly.

Tamra gazed into his eyes and luxuriated in the love she could feel emanating from him. She turned again to look at the view and had to admit, "There's only one thing that causes me any grief, and there's simply nothing I can do about it."

"Would you be talking about your mother?"

"Yeah." She sighed and leaned her elbows on the rail. "I've gotten beyond any ill feelings toward her; I really have. It would just be nice to . . . feel like she actually cared about me now, as an adult." She sighed again. "I can't help wondering if she will even read the card I sent, yet I can't help hoping that she will want to keep it . . . and that it might actually mean something to her."

Tamra turned her back to the rail and laid her head against Jess's shoulder. "But I may never know, so I just need to force it out of my mind and concentrate on all that I have to be grateful for." She looked up at him and he smiled. "And that's a lot."

* * *

Life became delightfully busy as Christmas preparations mingled with wedding plans. Jess spent a great deal of time in front of the computer, working to get ahead on his studies. Tamra worked with Emily and Sadie to decorate the house for Christmas, loving the magical feeling that surrounded her as they wove garlands around every stair railing, and hung a wreath on nearly every door. Tamra went with Jess and Michael up into the hills to cut two Christmas trees, one for the house, and another for the boys' home. She went with them to deliver the tree to the home, and was moved to tears to see how excited the boys became when they saw the tree arrive. Many of them greeted her with hugs and smiles, and she realized how much she missed working there. The temporary position she'd held had been filled, but she hoped that once she returned from her honeymoon and settled in, they would be able to find something for her to do here. Instinctively, she believed that working with these boys was simply meant to be.

Tamra awoke one morning with the idea of beginning a new Christmas tradition. She spoke with Emily about it, then e-mailed Claudia to get her recipe for the braided bread they'd made together. Emily and Tamra made it together, pleased that it turned out rather well. Admiring the result, Emily commented, "Now you've taken something you learned from your stepmother that you can do each year. Your children will grow up loving braided bread for Christmas, and they will make it for their children."

Tamra smiled and nodded, unable to explain why she suddenly felt so emotional over baking something. Perhaps it was more than that.

In the midst of decorating the house and baking Christmas goodies, wedding preparations moved along smoothly. Emily took Tamra to town to order a wedding gown and flowers. And since Jess had told his mother weeks ago to plan a celebration much like they had done for his siblings, Michael and Emily had already arranged a great deal. The wedding would take place in the Sydney Temple, with a meal afterward at a hotel where family and friends would gather. Jess and Tamra would spend their wedding night in Sydney, then honeymoon for a week before a reception would be held here at the house. Emily asked Tamra many questions about the arrangements she'd made, to be certain that she agreed with her decisions.

"It's not too late to change anything," Emily said. "If you don't like something, you need to speak up."

"I'm marrying Jess," Tamra said eagerly. "Anything else is just frosting on the cake."

Since they'd been talking about wedding cake, they both laughed, then moved on to other things.

It was a thrill to receive letters from Brady and Claudia, as well as copies of pictures they'd taken during their early Christmas celebration. Tamra picked up a photo album in town to put the pictures in, feeling peace with the idea of the new legacy she was beginning for her own children.

Tamra quickly became comfortable with Evelyn again, taking up the role she had established earlier of helping care for her off and on through the days. But now her interest was more defined, as Jess's was when he would take breaks from his studies and spend time with his little niece. As far as Tamra knew, nothing had been said to anyone else about their intentions, but Tamra felt certain that Michael and Emily could see the obvious solution. And with time it would all come together. Once they were married, they would proceed with the adoption process. Of course, there was no need for Evelyn to be sealed to them. She was sealed to her parents, and she would be with them again when this life was done. But for now, she would be theirs to love and raise as their own.

Christmas Eve arrived so quickly that it took Tamra's breath away to realize she would be married in less than two weeks. As she immersed herself into the traditions of this wonderful family, she realized that little had changed in the celebrations held in this house for decades. She'd read in family journals of providing Christmas for the boys in the home, and sharing dinner with them on Christmas Eve. Still, Tamra had never imagined how perfectly magical it felt to walk behind the horse-drawn wagon, piled with food and gifts, headed toward the boys' home. Jess held her hand, and Evelyn ran along beside them, giggling and talking of Father Christmas.

Tamra wasn't surprised to find that much of their celebration with the boys took place in the gabled attic. The room was reputed for being almost magical, and Tamra knew that it had been built as a symbol of another gabled attic that had been deeply significant to Jess and Alexa Byrnehouse-Davies, the founders of the home—Jess's great-great-grandparents.

While the boys were playing with the gifts Father Christmas had given them, Tamra stood before a plaque on the wall, recalling clearly when it had been put there at her suggestion. She had found the entry in Alexa's journal that explained the purpose behind this room, and she felt it would be appropriate to have her words posted here. Reading her words now sent chills through Tamra; they seemed to take on new meaning in light of all that had happened since she'd left here.

By looking east through the gabled window, we found the answers that eventually made it possible to merge the Byrnehouse and Davies names, and to have the means to fulfill Jess's dream of helping boys with no control over the circumstances that have marred their precious spirits. For us, the source of pain is deep and personal, as it is with every human being who fights to rise above the difficulties of this world to make something meaningful and rich of their lives. My deepest prayer is that every boy who has the opportunity to stand at these gabled windows and watch the sun rise will leave here changed for the better and more capable of finding a life of happiness and peace.

Tamra wiped the tears from her face, grateful that everyone else in the room was distracted. She turned to look out the window, where a dusky evening light glowed. She realized that for her, Alexa's prayer had been answered. She had not come here expecting great changes to take place within herself, but they had. She *had* become more capable of finding a life of peace and happiness. And she was grateful.

Through the remainder of the evening and the following day, as their Christmas celebrations continued, Tamra marveled at the sweet spirit filling the house and penetrating her heart and soul. She thought of the celebration she and Jess had shared with her father and stepmother. While it had been truly wonderful, Tamra couldn't deny the difference she felt here as their celebrations so strongly revolved around the Savior: His birth, His life, and all He had done. Thinking through the personal healing that both she and Jess had experienced, she doubted that Christmas could ever mean more to her than it did then. Fingering the little star hanging round her neck, she gazed up at the star atop the Christmas tree: *a guiding light through the darkness.* That's what Christmas was all about.

As Christmas day came to a close, Tamra lay in her bed, staring toward the ceiling as she contemplated her deepening happiness. But still, there was that one little ache in regard to her mother. If only she could know that her offering of love and forgiveness had been accepted. She reminded herself that it didn't matter how her mother had responded, only that she had done all she could do. Still, it would be nice to know.

The following morning, Tamra woke late and went downstairs in her bathrobe to find the family just finishing breakfast. Jess paused in washing Evelyn's hands and face to kiss Tamra quickly.

"How are you this morning?" he asked.

"Great, and you?"

"Great," he said and chuckled. Tamra thought nothing of his laughter until he exchanged a conspiratorial glance with each of his parents, who were still sitting at the table even though they'd finished eating.

"What?" she demanded.

"A package came for you a while ago," Michael said.

"A package?" Tamra echoed. "But the mail doesn't come until—"

"No, this was delivered FedEx," Emily explained, and walked into the other room to return with a large box.

Tamra's heart quickened as Michael quickly cleared a place on the table and Emily set the package there. It certainly was addressed to her, and she wondered for a moment if her father had sent something, in spite of the gifts they had exchanged last month. Then she saw the return address and gasped.

"Good heavens," she muttered and sank into a chair.

"Don't hyperventilate," Jess said. "Just open it. We can't stand it any longer."

Tamra forced herself to breathe deeply. "It doesn't matter what's inside," she said. "It's just . . . a miracle that she sent anything at all." She let out a breathless laugh. "I just can't believe it."

"Okay," Jess said, "it *is* a miracle. But *open* it!"

Tamra stood and opened the box with trembling hands, wondering what her mother might have sent her. Inside the FedEx box she found another box wrapped in Christmas paper, and a card in a red envelope. Holding the card in her hands, emotion bubbled out of her like an erupting volcano. It didn't matter what the card said. The very fact that she'd sent a card—and a *package*—already meant more to Tamra than she could ever say. Jess put his arms around Tamra and let her cry for a few minutes until Evelyn tugged on her bathrobe and asked, "You sad, Mama?"

"No, sweetie bug. I'm very happy. Shall we see what the card says?"

Tamra sat down and pulled Evelyn onto her lap. The child helped tear open the envelope and Tamra pulled out the card. It had a Victorian winter scene on the front, and the printed message inside simply said: *May your days be merry and bright.* And below that, in her mother's hand, was written: *Thank you for the card. It was good to see you again. Merry Christmas. Mom.*

Tamra started to cry again and handed the card to Jess for him to read while Evelyn tried to wipe Tamra's tears and comfort her.

"It's okay," Tamra said to her, noticing a distinct glisten of moisture in Jess's eyes. *It truly was a miracle!* She felt her testimony of the spirit of Elijah deepen with this tangible evidence of how her mother's heart had softened.

"May I?" Emily asked. Tamra nodded and Jess handed her the card. Michael looked over her shoulder so they could both read it. "Oh, that's beautiful," Emily said, her voice quavering. "It's perfect."

"Yes, it is," Tamra said and sniffled.

"Well, open the package," Jess insisted.

"I can't even guess," Tamra said and urged Evelyn to help her. She'd gotten a great deal of practice at opening gifts the previous morning, and she quickly tore the wrapping paper away. Tamra gasped when she saw what it was, then she laughed until she started to cry again.

Michael was obviously baffled. "An Easy-Bake Oven?" he asked.

"I'll tell you later, Dad," Jess said and wrapped his arms around Tamra, letting her cry some more. But Tamra doubted that anyone could ever put into words what this meant to her. She never would have dreamed that her mother would remember how badly she had wanted this as a child. The gift said more than words ever could that her mother was trying to somehow make up for some of the hurts of the past. And Tamra couldn't deny that it had worked.

Tamra finally managed to eat some breakfast, in spite of the delightful tremors going through her each time she glanced at the gift her mother had sent. She really didn't know what a woman her age would do with an Easy-Bake Oven, but she did know she would treasure it always.

* * *

Tamra walked down the hall toward the front of the house, with Evelyn's hand in hers. They found Jess in the lounge room, lying back on the sofa with a book.

"There you are," Tamra said as Evelyn climbed onto his lap even before he sat up. "We have a surprise for you."

"Really?" Jess said. "And what might that be?"

"You just have to come see," Tamra said and held out her hand.

They walked together out to the veranda, where Jess stopped and stared at the tiny little chocolate cake sitting in the center of the table, with toy dishes set out for three.

"Tell Daddy what we did," Tamra said to Evelyn.

"We baked a cake fo you," Evelyn said, climbing onto a chair. "We gonna have a tea pahty."

"So we are," Jess said, sitting beside Evelyn. "That's not a very big cake," he said, and Tamra laughed as she cut it into three pieces, as if it were fine French cuisine.

"No, but I'm sure it will taste great. I mean . . . when I was a kid and I'd see the commercials for these things, I just knew whatever I could bake would taste great."

"It *is* chocolate," Jess observed. Tamra just laughed and took his hand as she sat beside him. She didn't believe life could be any better than this.

About the Author

Anita Stansfield has been writing for more than twenty years, and her best-selling novels have captivated and moved hundreds of thousands of readers with their deeply romantic stories and focus on important contemporary issues. Her interest in creating romantic fiction began in high school, and her work has appeared in national publications. *Gables of Legacy: A Guiding Star* is her twenty-first novel to be published by Covenant.

Anita lives with her husband, Vince, and their five children and two cats in Alpine, Utah.